Other books by Lois Lowry:

The One Hundredth Thing About Caroline

Your Move, J.P.!

Anastasia Krupnik

Anastasia Again!

Autumn Street

The Silent Boy

Just the Tates!

Book 2

SWITCHAROUND

by LOIS LOWRY

HOUGHTON MIFFLIN HARCOURT

BOSTON NEW YORK

Book design by Rebecca Bond and Monica Liaw.
The text of this book is set in Adobe Garamond Pro.

The Library of Congress has cataloged the hardcover edition as follows:
Lowry, Lois.
Switcharound.
Summary: Forced to spend a summer with their father and his "new" family,
Caroline, age eleven, and J.P., age thirteen, are given unpleasant responsibilities
for which they are determined to get revenge.
[1. Brothers and sisters — Fiction. 2. Family life — Fiction. 3. Humorous stories.
I. Title. II: Title: Switch around.
Switcharound.
PZ7.L9673Sw 1985 [Fic] 85–14576

ISBN: 978-0-395-39536-3 hardcover
ISBN: 978-1-328-75087-7 paperback

Printed in the United States
DOC 10 9 8 7 6 5 4 3 2 1
4500695179

For Alix and Nick

ONE

"HE WANTS US TO DO *WHAT?*" Caroline Tate and her brother, J.P., spoke in unison. That was a very rare occurrence. Caroline and J.P. were such enemies that they usually never spoke at all in each other's presence; now, suddenly, they were not only speaking, but saying exactly the same thing. And then they did it a second time. "HE WANTS US TO DO *WHAT?*" they asked again.

Their mother looked at them in amazement. "You two should try out for the Mormon Tabernacle Choir," she said.

"Don't change the subject, Mom," Caroline said. "Let me see the letter. I can't believe I heard you correctly. It's a cruel hoax, right?" She reached over and took the letter that her mother was holding.

Caroline read it quickly; it was a short letter. "I can't speak," she said when she had finished. "I'm just sitting here in stunned silence."

"Lemme look," said her brother, and he took the letter. J.P. was such a genius and speed-reader that he only needed to glance at it and he had it memorized. "I can speak," he announced. "No. I won't go."

Joanna Tate looked at them both and sighed. "It's a shock, isn't it? After all these years. I don't blame you guys for being upset. I guess I am, too. But you know, maybe it's not such a bad idea after all—"

"On a bad-idea scale, from one to ten," said J.P., "with nuclear war rated ten, *this* idea would come in at a good eight."

"Nine," said Caroline. "I think it's a nine. And I won't go, either. For the first time in my life I agree with J.P."

"Hold it," their mother said. "There's something you don't understand."

"Wrong," Caroline said. "I understand perfectly. You and he were divorced when I was two years old—that's nine years ago—and J.P. was four. He never writes to us. For Christmas and birthdays he spends a whole lot of time and thought renewing our magazine subscriptions—"

"His *secretary* renews the subscriptions," J.P. interrupted.

"You like those magazines," their mother pointed out.

"The point is," Caroline went on, "he doesn't really care anything about us. *Twice* we went there to visit—twice in nine years—and both times it was just for a week, and both times it was *boring*. And now he says he wants us for a whole summer? No way."

"I have plans for this summer," J.P. added. "I plan to build a computer this summer."

"I don't have any particular plans," Caroline admitted. "But I sure am going to *come up* with some plans, and they are not going to include Des Moines, Iowa."

"Well," said Joanna Tate, looking miserable,

"believe me, I understand how you feel. But I have to be honest with you. You *are* going to Des Moines for the summer. Both of you. There's nothing I can do about it."

"WHY NOT?" bellowed Caroline and J.P. together.

"Because," she explained, "our divorce agreement says that he can have you for the summer. It says *every* summer, in fact. But it was never convenient for him before. One summer he had a girlfriend living there. And one summer he was playing on a softball team. One summer he had a cold. And one summer he had just gotten married. And the next summer his wife had just had a baby. And one summer—oh, I forget. He always had an excuse."

She crumpled the letter and stared out the window, down into the New York street at the people, cars, noise, and bustle. "It might be *fun* to spend a summer away from the city," she suggested. "I've never been able to afford to send you to camp or anything. And I worry about you when I'm at work and school's out."

Caroline and J.P. stared at her and didn't say anything.

"It might be fun," their mother said again, very glumly. But she said it the way someone would say, "This might be good," about a tuna fish and bean sprout casserole. Polite. Hopeful, even. But not convinced.

"Mom," Caroline said finally. "If the law says I have to go, then I'll go. I'm not going to run away or anything. How about you, J.P.? Were you thinking of running away?"

"No," said J.P. "Actually, I was thinking that I might handcuff myself to the doorknob of my bedroom and then swallow the key to the handcuffs."

"But how could you build your computer if you were handcuffed to a doorknob?"

"There's a problem there," J.P. acknowledged.

"Can J.P. take all his electronics stuff to Des Moines?" Caroline asked her mother.

"Actually, I was assuming he would. Even *hoping* he would, so that I can clean his room for the first time in five years."

"J.P.," asked Caroline, "if you could take all your electronics gear, would you go? Because I guess I'm going, but I don't want to go alone."

"If you get him to sign a paper that I won't have to play baseball," J.P. said. "I want a legal statement, notarized and everything. Last time I visited him he kept making me play baseball. He called me 'fella' all the time. I want it to say in the statement that he won't call me 'fella.'"

"That's right!" Caroline said. "I'd forgotten that! And he called me 'princess'! He couldn't ever remember our real names! Make him promise not to call me 'princess,' Mom!"

Joanna Tate nodded. "I'll call him," she said. "And you two can talk to him and tell him all of that. Write out a list of requests—like no baseball, and no stupid nicknames—and you can negotiate that over the phone.

"I wish I'd been as assertive as you kids are," she added, "when he and I were married. Because—well, you want to hear something really disgusting?"

Caroline and J.P. nodded.

"He used to call me Jo-Jo," their mother confessed, cringing.

"See?" said Caroline and J.P., like the Mormon Tabernacle Choir. "SEE?"

Caroline kicked the bedpost in frustration. She was packing. Or at least she was *trying* to pack. Packing was hard enough normally for someone who had never traveled very much. But packing to visit her father in Des Moines? Impossible.

How could someone who had lived in New York City since she was two years old possibly pack to go to Des Moines? What kind of city was Des Moines, anyway? It wasn't even pronounced the way it looked.

"You can't trust a city that doesn't pronounce its final consonants," Caroline muttered to her stuffed stegosaurus. She put him into a corner of the big suitcase, next to her folded pajamas.

What did people wear in Des Moines? Farm overalls? Tough. She didn't have any.

Dejectedly, Caroline peered into her closet.

School had ended for the year, but her school clothes were still hanging there: navy blue jumpers and white blouses, the official girls' uniform at the Burke-Thaxter School. J.P. wore a white shirt, with chinos, and a blue tie. They each had navy blue blazers with a B-T emblem on the pocket.

No *way* was she going to take her B-T blazer to Des Moines. Caroline was no dummy, and she knew what would happen if she did. Big Turkey, the other kids would call her. That's what rival schools always said about Burke-Thaxter.

Other kids. The phrase made her stomach churn. Would there *be* any other kids in Des Moines? Would she make friends? Because if not, she'd be stuck with J.P. all summer. And she and J.P. had hated each other since they were toddlers.

Her father and his second wife did have a little boy, she remembered. When she had visited last, for a week, the little boy—What was his name? Something stupid, but she couldn't think of it—was just little, maybe about three. And that had been three years ago. So now he—Butchie? Was that it? Dutchie?—would be about six. A horrible age.

8

She took her stuffed stegosaurus out of the suitcase. That bratty little Butchie or Kootchy or Whoever would probably find him and destroy him—good old Steg, who had seen Caroline through some very stressful times. Maybe he should stay in New York for the summer.

She packed all of her jeans and one dress. Underwear. A sweater. Some shirts.

She opened the bedroom door and called to her mother. "Should I pack my bathing suit?"

It was J.P. who answered from his bedroom, where he was also packing. "Don't bother," he called back. "They're always having droughts out there. It's all dead cattle bones lying around in deserts. There's no place to go swimming."

But Joanna Tate appeared, drying her hands on a kitchen towel. "Don't be silly, James," she said. "Sure, Caroline, pack your bathing suit. There'll be a pool somewhere. No ocean, of course, but I'm sure there will be a pool. Or at least they'll have a sprinkler you can run through."

Caroline sighed and tossed her blue bathing suit into the suitcase. She hoped they didn't have a

"What I Did on My Vacation" assignment for English class in the fall, because if her composition said, "I ran through a sprinkler in Des Moines with my half brother Butchie (or Dutchie, or Kootchy, or Something)," she would be laughed out of Burke-Thaxter School.

Caroline's very best friend, Stacy Baurichter, was going to sailing camp in Maine. And one of her very worst enemies in school, Ruthie Pierce-Donnelly, was spending part of the summer at a special science program for gifted children at Yale University. Boy, talk about showoffs; Caroline wouldn't have been at all surprised if Ruthie had had cards printed: RUTH ELLEN PIERCE-DONNELLY, GIFTED CHILD.

J.P. was gifted, too, thought Caroline, even if he was obnoxious. He could have gotten in to the special thing at Yale; they had said so at school. They had said he should apply. But it cost a lot, and Joanna Tate couldn't afford it.

She couldn't even afford the plane tickets to Des Moines. But their father had sent them. Tourist class, of course.

Caroline tossed some socks into the suitcase. She added her books and poked everything so that it fit and the lid would close.

"There. I'm all packed, I guess," she said gloomily to no one in particular.

J.P. heard her. "Me too," he said, equally gloomily, and came to stand in her doorway. "I packed all my transformers and batteries and wires, and my tool set, and a broken radio that I'm working on, and some diodes and electrodes and cathodes and some computer components, and—" He looked suddenly over at Caroline's suitcase.

"Oh," he said and turned to go back to his bedroom. "I forgot clothes."

Two

"Pretend you don't know me," J.P. said. "I want to walk by myself. I don't want people to know I'm with you guys. Especially with *her*," he added, gesturing toward his sister.

"Jerk," Caroline said.

Their mother frowned. "James," she said, "walk by yourself if you want to. But keep us in sight, okay? This is a huge airport, and I don't want to lose you. The flight is number eight-nine-two, and it leaves at one-thirty from gate forty-five. Do you both have everything? The stubs for the checked luggage are stapled to your tickets. Do you both have your tickets?"

Caroline opened her pocketbook and showed her ticket to her mother. J.P. was looking the other way, pretending he'd never seen them before in his life. But his ticket was visible, the end of it appearing at his jacket pocket.

"Are you sure you don't want to check that bag?" Joanna Tate asked him. "It looks heavy."

"I told you," J.P. muttered. "It's my valuable stuff." He shifted the small suitcase from one hand to the other. It made a clanking noise.

"It's all his tools," Caroline explained to her mother. "Plus a dumb broken radio and a busted clock that he found in a trash can on Eighty-Second Street."

J.P. glared at her angrily. "Why don't you print up announcements about my personal life, Caroline?" he asked sarcastically. "Maybe you could stand on a street corner and distribute them."

Their mother shook her head. "I hope you two will outgrow this warfare," she said. She looked at her watch. "Okay. Onward. James, from now on we'll pretend we don't know you. But don't you *dare* wander off and get lost."

J.P. had shifted his clanking suitcase again and started off. Caroline walked behind him, with her mother. She had an odd desire, suddenly, to hold her mother's hand. But she resisted it. She was eleven years old, after all—almost an adult. She was just as tall as her brother, who was thirteen.

Around them, crowds moved purposefully, all of them streaming toward various gates and stairs and doors. Babies cried. Couples kissed goodbye or hello. Uniformed pilots with wings on their chests strode along the corridors without looking left or right. Flight attendants pulled their little wheeled carts of luggage and chatted together as they moved along.

Caroline and her mother watched as J.P. stopped in front of a machine, set his clanking suitcase down, and reached into his pocket for some change. "He's buying *cigarettes!*" Caroline whispered to her mother.

Her mother chuckled. "No, he's not. It's a candy

machine. Don't stare at him, Caroline. He hates that. Come on—we'll walk ahead, as if we don't know him."

At the entrance to the departure gates, Caroline and her mother put their pocketbooks onto the moving belt of the x-ray machine and walked through the metal detector. When they picked their bags back up, Caroline glanced behind her and saw J.P. waiting in line to go through the security devices. He was munching on a candy bar.

"He's still there," she reassured her mother. "He didn't get lost."

Together they walked on toward gate 45. At each gate they could read the destinations of the airplanes. San Francisco. Denver. Honolulu. If only her father lived in Honolulu, Caroline thought; *then* she wouldn't mind visiting him for the summer. Heck, she'd even visit him for the *winter* if he lived in Honolulu.

"Now," said her mother, as they reached gate 45, "your boarding pass is with your ticket. And I hate to tell you this, but you and your brother are sitting next to each other."

"Who gets the window?" Caroline asked suspiciously.

"I can't remember which one has the window seat. But you can switch halfway there, to make it fair. Where *is* J.P.?" Joanna Tate peered down the long corridor. "I thought he was right behind us."

"Listen!" Caroline grabbed her mother's arm. "They said your name."

They listened. Sure enough, the public-address system was saying in its monotonous voice, "Joanna Tate. Please report to the security checkpoint."

Caroline trotted along beside her mother as they hurried back to the place where they had last seen J.P. waiting in line. And there he still was. But he was surrounded by a cluster of uniformed airport officials. His pockets were turned inside out, and the contents—a jackknife, some small screwdrivers, and a pair of needlenose pliers—were in front of him on a tray. They were the things J.P. *always* carried in his pocket; Caroline knew that because when she did the laundry, she sometimes had to dump them out if he had forgotten.

In front of him, on a table, his small suitcase was

open. Two men were examining the contents, and their faces were grim. Carefully they removed the broken alarm clock that J.P. had retrieved from a trash can. Then they took out the radio with the missing dials. One man poked suspiciously at the tangle of wires that protruded from a pocket of the suitcase.

"What's the trouble?" asked Joanna Tate in a worried voice.

"Mom!" said J.P. "That's my mom and my sister," he explained to the men, in relief.

"Gentlemen," announced Caroline loudly, "we have never seen this person before in our lives."

J.P. stared at the clouds. Beside him, Caroline stared at the back of the seat in front of her. Finally she turned to her brother.

"You'll get it back," she said. "They said you'd get it back in Des Moines. It was only that you couldn't carry it on the plane. It's down with our other suitcases."

J.P. frowned. "I know," he said. "But it's all my valuable stuff. And you sure weren't any help,

Caroline. For a minute I thought they were going to haul me off to jail."

"I said I was sorry," Caroline told him.

A flight attendant appeared beside their seats. "Want anything to drink?" she asked.

Caroline and J.P. took two ginger ales and sipped.

"I *am* sorry, too," Caroline admitted finally. "I'm sorry I did that, back at the gate. You know what, J.P.?"

"What?" He stirred his ice cubes with a straw.

"I've been thinking. You and I have always been enemies, right?"

"Right."

"At home we're always plotting rotten things to do to each other," Caroline pointed out.

J.P. nodded. He grinned. "Like the time I hot-wired the coat hangers in your closet so that every time you reached for something to wear, you got a shock."

"Exactly," Caroline acknowledged, remembering the incident. "And then I hid a centerfold from *Playboy* inside your math book so when you opened your book in class, Miss October popped out, and Mr. Jacobsen made you stay after school and explain—"

"Yeah, that was really stupid, Caroline. I don't even *like* girls. The only thing I like in *Playboy* is the science fiction and the car stuff. Remember how I got even? I wired up that burglar alarm on your locker at school so when you opened it to get your books out—"

"Right. And then I—Wait a minute, J.P. Let me tell you what I was thinking. I was thinking that in Des Moines, you and I shouldn't waste a lot of valuable time being enemies. We should maybe take a summer vacation from being enemies. We should team up."

"What do you mean, team up? You're not going to try to get me to play baseball, Caroline—"

"No, no," Caroline reassured him. "I just meant we should stick together. Because there will be *other* enemies in Des Moines."

"Dad, for one," said J.P. gloomily. "If he calls me 'fella' just once—just *once*—"

"And his wife. I can't remember her name. She

wasn't so bad, but she's always on his side," Caroline said.

"His wife's name is Lillian. Don't forget that I have a photographic memory, Caroline. Anything you want remembered, just ask me."

"Their kid. That obnoxious little kid. He had some weird name—what was it?" Caroline asked. "Was it Butchie?"

J.P. choked on the last piece of ice. He sputtered, laughing. "You can't remember the kid's name?"

"No. Dutchy?"

J.P. doubled over. "I'm not going to tell you. Wait till you find out, though. They'll be at the airport, and the kid will be there, and Dad will say something like, 'You remember our son—' and you wait, Caroline, you *see* if you can keep a straight face. I *dare* you to keep a straight face."

Caroline sighed. "I'm pretty good at straight faces," she said. "Anyway, you see what I mean, J.P.? It's you and me against *them*. So I think we ought to call off our own war, just for the summer."

"Détente," announced J.P.

"What?"

"You ought to pay more attention in school, Caroline," he said. "Or read the newspapers. When two countries that have been enemies decide to try being friends, it's called détente."

"Like the United States and Russia?" Caroline asked.

J.P. nodded. "We might as well try it," he said.

"The Tate Détente," Caroline pronounced. "It sounds pretty impressive."

"You want to shake hands?" her brother asked.

She looked at him suspiciously. "You don't have your hands hot-wired, do you, so I'll get a shock?"

J.P. exhibited his hands, palms up. "They took all my electronic equipment away, remember?"

Caroline shook his hand solemnly. Then she giggled suddenly when she thought of something.

"I have a toast," she said, and held up her empty ginger ale glass. J.P. tapped his glass against hers.

"To us," Caroline announced. "To the United Tates of America!"

THREE

"YOU WON'T BE ABLE TO MISS OUR CAR," Herbert Tate announced as he carried the two suitcases across the parking lot. The gleaming parked cars all shimmered in the bright sunlight. It was so hot that the asphalt was steaming, and the air seemed blurred in front of Caroline's eyes.

Of course, she had a particular problem that might be affecting her eyes. She was still trying to keep a straight face. She had told J.P. that she was pretty good at straight faces. And she *was*, ordinarily. But this was an unusual situation. When her father had said, as Caroline and J.P. got off the plane, "You remember our son —" and then gone on to say it — out loud — that *name* — well, she had been having a very tough time, ever since, with her face. She was having to bite the inside of her lips very hard.

"Why?" asked J.P. He was walking beside Caroline, clutching his clanking suitcase. "Why won't we be able to miss your car? I don't even know what kind of car you have." Then he stopped walking and stood still. "Oh," he said. "I see what you mean."

Caroline stopped, too, and looked. The car was a gray station wagon — nothing extraordinary about that. But it was covered with writing. On the driver's door, it said, in dark red letters: MAKE A DATE WITH HERBIE TATE.

On the door behind that: MEET YOUR FATE AT HERBIE TATE.

Silently, Caroline and J.P. walked around to the other side of the station wagon and looked. On one door: DON'T BE LATE FOR HERBIE TATE.

And on the other: WE'RE CUT-RATE AT HERBIE TATE.

Across the back of the car, in larger letters, it said simply: HERBIE TATE'S SPORTING GOODS.

Caroline's face failed. She couldn't bite the inside of her lips anymore. She started to giggle. She glanced at her brother. J.P. wasn't a giggler; he didn't even *laugh* very often. But he glanced back at Caroline and lost control of himself. He set his suitcase down in the parking lot and doubled over, clutching his stomach. Together Caroline and J.P. laughed until tears appeared on their cheeks. When, breathless, they finally managed to stop, they saw that Herbie and Lillian Tate were grinning proudly at them.

"You like it, huh?" said their father. He opened the back—HERBIE TATE'S SPORTING GOODS—and put their suitcases inside. "Lillian just had it done, as a surprise for my birthday. Her uncle's a sign painter."

"He would have painted footballs and baseballs and basketballs all over, but I thought that would be too much," Lillian explained.

"We'll have to have it all redone in a few years," Herbie Tate said as he lifted his little boy, who was sucking his thumb, into the back seat. "When my boy gets old enough to come into the business, then we'll have new signs. Right, fella?" He tickled his son under the chin, and the little boy nodded, still sucking noisily on his glistening thumb.

"And the new signs will say—" Herbie Tate went on. Then he stopped and gestured to Caroline and J.P., so that they could guess the ending.

"HERBIE AND POOCHIE TATE'S SPORTING GOODS," they said together, and bit their lips so that they wouldn't break up again.

"Come on," called Lillian from the front seat. "Let's go home!"

Caroline and J.P. climbed into the back of the station wagon beside the little boy, whose curly hair was damp with sweat. He glanced over at them shyly. Finally he removed his thumb from his mouth and revealed missing front teeth. "Hi," he said nervously, the way you might say "hi" to someone who had just appeared in a dark alley, pointing a gun in your direction.

"Hi, Poochie," Caroline replied. She felt a little

sorry for someone who was so terrified and who had to be named Poochie, as well. She also felt a little sorry for herself.

The car moved along through the streets, which were very, very different from the familiar streets of New York. Caroline pushed her hair back under her headband with a moist hand and watched through the windows. Shopping centers. Schools. Churches. Apartment complexes. And more shopping centers, shopping centers, shopping centers. Apparently people in Des Moines did nothing but go shopping.

"There's a Radio Shack, J.P.," she whispered, pointing. He nodded. But he looked as if he felt just as depressed as Caroline did.

"I'd take you by the store," their father said, turning to glance at them from the front seat as he drove, "but it's a little out of the way. And everything's a mess there this week, anyway. I know you saw it when you were here last—when was that? Two years ago?"

"Three," Caroline said. "It was three years ago."

"Well, we've expanded a lot since then. We used to be strictly sports equipment. But now we've branched out into clothes, too—sports clothes, you know? Tennis outfits, jogging wear, even shoes. We have a whole line of shoes. Maybe you kids could do with some jogging shoes while you're here. What do you think?"

Caroline smiled politely, even though her father's head was turned back to watch the road, so he couldn't see her smile. One of the sayings on the door of the car came to her mind. MEET YOUR FATE WITH HERBIE TATE. That's what I've done, thought Caroline; I've met my fate. My fate is to spend the summer with people who want me to wear jogging shoes.

She felt hideously depressed. Through the windows of the car, more shopping centers and shopping plazas and shopping malls whizzed past. Where were the museums? In New York, Caroline spent all her time at the Museum of Natural History. It was her favorite place in the entire world. And this July they were going to be having an entire special week devoted to primates: lectures, movies, famous people in primate research visiting and showing slides. Since it wasn't during the school year, Caroline would have been able to go. She would have been able to spend a whole week learning more about primates.

If she weren't in Des Moines, that is. Trying on jogging shoes.

"Almost there," announced Herbie Tate.

"J.P.," Lillian said, turning around to look toward the back seat. "We've put you in Poochie's room—there are bunk beds. I hope you won't mind having the top; Pooch is afraid of the height."

Poochie slumped farther down into the seat, looking humiliated, his mouth working around his thumb. J.P. just stared morosely at Lillian Tate. Caroline knew exactly what he was thinking and feeling. All of his electronics gear. J.P. had been planning to survive the summer in Des Moines by shutting himself in his room and working with his tools and wires and batteries. How could he do that if he didn't even have a room of his own?

At least, thought Caroline with some grim satisfaction, I don't have to share a room with them. I'll have a room of my own, and I can *read* all summer.

She had brought with her, in her suitcase, almost more books than clothes. She began trying to recall their titles: *The Clan of the Cave Bear* (one of her favorites; she was going to read it for the second time), *An Anthropologist's Life, Primitive Man,* and—

Caroline's thoughts were interrupted when Herbie Tate swung the big car around a corner of the residential street. He pulled into a driveway leading to a garage. Next to the garage was an ordinary-looking brick house. Caroline stared. Herbie and his wife had moved since she had visited before, and this house was one she had never seen. But it had an odd, familiar look to it.

She poked her brother. "*Leave It to Beaver?*" she murmured.

J.P. stared at the house. "*My Three Sons?*" he responded.

"*Father Knows Best? The Donna Reed Show?*" Caroline suggested.

"All of the above," J.P. announced as he picked up his small suitcase from the floor of the car.

Caroline was staring at something she couldn't quite believe on the front lawn of the TV sitcom *Leave It to Beaver* house. How interesting, she thought: a mirage. The heat has created a mirage right here in Des Moines, the way it creates mirages on the desert. I wonder if J.P. is also seeing it, or if it is a single-person mirage. Suddenly she became aware that Lillian, still looking over the back seat, was talking to her.

"And we've put you in with the girls, Caroline," Lillian was saying.

Caroline blinked. "The girls?" she asked politely. "Who are the girls?"

Lillian Tate looked startled. "The babies," she said as if that were an explanation. "Didn't your mother tell you about the babies?"

"I don't think I ever mentioned to Joanna that we'd had the twins," Herbie said to his wife. "She and I don't really stay in touch, you know."

Caroline looked again at the mirage. It was a

huge double baby carriage parked on the lawn. "No," Caroline said with a sinking feeling, a realization that Des Moines didn't have mirages after all. "I didn't know about the twins. And you, ah, said I'd be sharing their room?"

Lillian Tate smiled pleasantly. "We put a nice bed in there for you," she said. "It fits right between the cribs."

FOUR

"DEAR MOM," WROTE CAROLINE that night, and then hesitated. How honest should she be? She didn't like to lie to her mother. And she knew that her mother was hoping that she and J.P. would have a good summer in Des Moines. And there was nothing that her mother could do about things, since the court said that they should spend the summers with their father.

She sighed, looked at the piece of paper, and sipped at the glass of lemonade Lillian had given her. It was still horribly hot, even though it was eight P.M.

"We arrived safely," she wrote.

"Did the plane arrive on time?" she asked, looking up from the table where she was writing. Lillian, Herbie, and J.P. were all watching television. Poochie and the babies were in bed.

"Right on time," Herbie told her. "Even a couple of minutes early."

"The plane was right on time," Caroline wrote, "and Dad and Lillian were there to meet us, with their little boy named Poochie.

"J.P. and I did not fight at all on the plane, not even about who got the window. In fact, we have not fought since we got here, either. We have decided to have an agreement to be friends, all summer.

"Mom, maybe you didn't know it, but Dad and Lillian had twin babies last December. Both girls. They look exactly alike, which means partially bald, with brown eyes. These babies were something of a surprise to me and J.P. since we didn't know about them in advance, and it was even a worse surprise to me than it was to J.P., because I have to sleep in the same room with them.

"Worse than that, Mom, I also am going to have to take care of them a lot, because it turns out that Lillian is going to spend the summer taking a real estate course so that she can become a person who sells houses. She's going to be gone almost all of every day. And I think that's just fine if Lillian wants to become a real estate person because I have nothing against real estate people, but, Mom, I have to tell you that I think it's pretty crummy that I have to become a person who takes care of babies.

"Remember when you and I had a long conversation once about marriage after I decided to become a paleontologist? Because paleontologists have to travel a lot, to places like Asia Minor, and so it would be hard to have a husband and harder still to have children? And remember I told you that I had decided that I probably would not ever want to get married and *definitely* did not want to have children, *ever?*

"Well, it doesn't seem fair that someone who has

already definitely decided that she doesn't want to have children should get stuck taking care of someone else's for the summer. I don't mean to be a bad sport, but I really wanted to go to the primate seminar at the Museum of Natural History in July. And instead I have to take care of these babies.

"I didn't even tell you their names. This, honestly, is *gross*. When Lillian brought them out, after we arrived from the airport (a babysitter had been with them), and J.P. and I said very politely how cute they were (we really were polite, Mom, I promise. And they AREN'T cute, not at all), I asked very politely what their names are. And Lillian said: 'GUESS.' Talk about stupid: I mean how are you supposed to guess not one, but two names? J.P. and I just stood there looking stupid and Lillian laughed and said: 'I'll give you a hint. They were born Christmas Day.'

"Right away J.P. guessed Mary and Joseph, which was really dumb because they are both girls. So then he guessed Frankincense and Myrrh, and everybody laughed, ha ha, and then he said he didn't want to guess anymore.

"Well, I didn't want to guess either, but I wanted

to get the conversation over with, because she had plunked one of the babies into my lap, and it was gnawing on my finger, and it hurt. (They each have two teeth, absolutely identical.) So I guessed Beth for Bethlehem, and Noel, and everybody agreed that that was clever, but it was wrong, too.

"And then Lillian explained that they are named Holly and Ivy, because there is a Christmas carol called 'The Holly and the Ivy,' which I never heard of, and she started to sing it, but fortunately one of the babies started to cry, and so she took them away to change their diapers.

"Anyway, that is all that has happened so far. J.P. has to sleep in Poochie's upper bunk, and I have to sleep between two cribs, surrounded by Holly and Ivy. So far Des Moines is not very much fun. But they have a huge color TV, and a big yard, and we don't have either of those in New York. And we had steak for dinner, which we don't have at home. So there are some okay parts.

"Love,

"Caroline"

She folded the pages, addressed the envelope,

and sealed the letter. Across the room, the TV flickered, a few gunshots came from the set, followed by music, and then a commercial began. Herbie Tate yawned and turned it off.

"Getting late," he announced. "Bedtime at the O.K. Corral. Lots of work to do on the old ranch tomorrow, right, Diamond Lil?" He poked Lillian in the side with his elbow. She nodded.

Caroline winced. Her father had a habit of making very stupid remarks, and if there was anything she couldn't stand, it was someone who poked other people in the side with an elbow.

"It's only nine o'clock," J.P. pointed out after he had looked at his watch. "I don't have to go to bed this early at home if it's not a school night. And what do you mean, lots to do? What do I have to do?"

His father grinned proudly. "I've lined up a big job for you this summer," he said.

Caroline could see J.P.'s shoulders stiffen. And even though they had agreed on the Tate Détente, that they wouldn't be enemies in Des Moines, she felt a little bit of satisfaction. When that repulsive baby had been set down on her lap earlier, and

Lillian had told her that she would be taking care of the "twinnies" this summer, she could see that J.P. was smirking.

At least they had planned something horrible for him, too.

"What is it?" J.P. asked, in the polite but suspicious voice that people usually reserve for unidentifiable vegetables on their plates.

Herbie Tate went to the closet and took out a package. "I had this made," he explained, "and now that I can see you in person, I can tell that I estimated your size wrong. Frankly, J.P., I thought that at thirteen you'd be bigger than you are. When I was thirteen, I had really well-developed biceps and pectorals. Of course, I was a true athlete."

Caroline watched J.P. and felt truly sorry for him. Poor scrawny J.P., who spent his entire life with computers and motors and chess sets and who never ever, if he could help it, engaged in any sport. Even at school, in gym, the coach let him be scorekeeper, stopwatch holder, towel distributor.

Now J.P. was simply staring at his father, who was demonstrating his biceps by squeezing one arm against his waist so that the muscle thickened and rippled, like a guy in a beer commercial.

"Take your shirt off, son," Herbie Tate commanded; and J.P., speechless for a change, obeyed. He pulled his T-shirt over his head, leaving his hair standing upright and his skinny chest, with its visible ribs, exposed.

"Here," said his father, "put this on." He tossed him the contents of the package, a bright blue shirt. J.P. pulled it down over his messed-up hair and pushed his arms through the sleeves.

It was huge. At least three sizes too big for skinny J.P. But it had his name in mammoth white letters across the back. J. P. TATE, it said. And below that: COACH.

"Meet your fate with Herbie Tate," Caroline murmured, but no one heard her.

"I told you," J.P. said at last, miserably, "I won't play baseball. I told you that on the phone. And you promised."

"Right," said Herbie Tate agreeably. "And you don't have to. But you're going to coach the Tater Chips."

40

"The WHAT?" J.P. asked.

"That's Poochie's baseball team. I've got them all outfitted — from the store, of course — in blue and white, just like you. And their first practice is at nine o'clock tomorrow morning. Twelve six-year-olds, down at the park."

Lillian, who had been collecting the lemonade glasses and the empty popcorn bowl, looked up suddenly as if she had a new idea. "Caroline," she said, "the park is only a couple of blocks away. After their morning nap, you can push the twins down there in their carriage. Then you can walk home with J.P. and Poochie in time to fix lunch."

"In time to fix lunch," Caroline repeated, because she couldn't think of anything else to say.

"I'll be at my morning classes," Lillian explained cheerfully. "I have to leave here real early in the morning. But I have all the babysitting instructions typed out for you."

J.P. was still standing in the center of the living room, with his thin, pale arms dangling from the enormous sleeves of the too-big blue shirt. "Twelve six-year-olds," he said in an I-don't-believe-this voice.

"Now," said Herbie Tate, "Taps." Caroline and J.P. watched in disbelief as he held up an imaginary bugle and blew the first few bars of "Taps": *da da dum; da da duuummmm.*

As they trudged down the carpeted hallway to their rooms, Lillian called after them in a very loud whisper, "Don't wake Poochie or the twins!"

J.P. turned to Caroline as he opened the door of his room. "This is all a bad dream, right?" he muttered. "We're in a nightmare."

"Wrong," Caroline said. "We're in Des Moines."

FIVE

IT WAS EARLY MORNING. There were strange sounds in the room, and for a moment Caroline couldn't remember where she was. She lay very still, with her eyes closed, and tried to think.

In New York, early on a summer morning, the sounds would be *Clank, Crash, Whack* (the trash men). And *Honk, Beep, Slam* (taxis). The shower, as her mother got ready to go to work. Maybe the *burble, burble, burble* of the coffeepot in the kitchen. The muted footsteps of the people in the upstairs apartment.

Here—wherever she was—the sounds were quieter and absolutely unidentifiable. A rhythmic *thump, thump, thump;* a slurpy, sucking sound; and a giggle. A giggle very close to her face.

Caroline opened her eyes. It all came back to her; she groaned, closed her eyes, and pulled the pillow over her head.

Des Moines. And babies.

A wet hand grabbed her hair and pulled. She couldn't escape. Reluctantly Caroline tossed the pillow aside and removed her hair carefully from the baby's chubby fingers. The baby giggled again, put the fist back into her own mouth, and made more slurping noises.

The other baby kicked the sides of her crib with little bare feet: *thump, thump, thump.*

Caroline looked gloomily from one to the other. On her left, in a pink crib, wearing a pink nightgown: that was Holly. On her right, in a yellow crib, wearing a yellow nightgown: that was Ivy. The colors were the way they told the identical babies apart. Not that Caroline cared.

She yawned and tried to remember the instructions that Lillian had given her.

Diapers. The giant box of disposable diapers was in the corner of the room. All the diapers were white. So it didn't matter who got which diaper, as long as they both got dry diapers in the morning.

Caroline looked from one baby to the other. "Are you guys wet?" she asked.

Are you guys wet. Is the pope Catholic? Caroline thought. What a dumb question. They were so wet she could hear them *squish* when they moved.

Sleepily she went to the diaper box, took out two diapers, and started in on the pink baby, Holly. Lillian had shown her, last night, how the diapers worked. But Holly kicked and giggled and grabbed at Caroline's hair.

"Cut it out," Caroline said grouchily. Finally she got the diaper firmly attached and pulled Holly's little pink nightgown back down. She dropped the wet diaper into the plastic container Lillian had shown her and then changed the yellow baby, Ivy. It went a little more smoothly the second time.

Caroline looked at her watch. Seven a.m. "I don't suppose you guys would like to go back to sleep for about an hour," she suggested. "This is my summer vacation."

But the babies just giggled again, thumping their cribs. One of them, the yellow one, got up on her hands and knees and bounced. Then she fell forward, bumped her chin, and began to cry. The pink baby cried sympathetically.

Caroline pulled on her bathrobe in disgust. "I just want you to know that I plan to remain childless, myself," she told the twins. They weren't paying any attention. They were wailing.

One at a time she carried them to the kitchen and deposited them unceremoniously into the big playpen. "Orange juice," she said aloud. That was the second thing on the babies' morning schedule, right after the dry diapers. In the refrigerator were two small bottles of orange juice that Lillian had prepared the night before. One had a pink plastic cap and one had a yellow plastic cap.

"It doesn't really matter," Lillian had explained

to Caroline, "because the juice is just the same. But it's a good idea just to stay in the yellow/pink habit."

"Here," Caroline said. She poked the yellow bottle into the yellow baby's mouth and waited while Ivy reached up and got a grip on it. Then she did the same with the pink bottle and the pink baby. The crying silenced. The bottles were like plugs.

Now that the babies were quiet, absorbed with their orange juice, Caroline flipped the switch on the TV and sank onto the couch near the playpen. Half asleep, she stared at some ancient cartoons and wondered if she would remember how to make the babies' oatmeal. The little pink bowl and the little yellow bowl were set out on the counter, waiting.

Poochie appeared, glanced at the twins in the playpen and then at Caroline, hitched up his drooping pajama pants, and went to the cupboard. Carefully he took out a bowl and a box of cereal. Then he went to the drawer for a spoon, to the cupboard for the sugar bowl, and to the refrigerator for a bottle of milk. He arranged everything precisely on the floor in front of the TV, plopped down, and put it all together for his breakfast.

Well, thought Caroline, at least I don't have to feed him, too.

She was beginning to feel more awake. In a minute she would start to make the babies' oatmeal. Their bottles were empty. Holly was whacking Ivy across the back with her empty bottle. Ivy wasn't paying any attention. She was trying to poke the nipple of hers into her ear.

"How are you doing, Pooch? You all ready for baseball practice?" Caroline asked.

Poochie grunted. He stirred his cereal and took another bite. "I hate baseball," he said with his mouth full. He stared at the cartoon on the television. "Roadrunner goes over the cliff," he said, "and lands on a train that's going past. I've seen this one a million times."

"Me too. But it's all news on the other channels." Caroline began to warm some milk in a shallow pan on the stove. She added the oatmeal and stirred until it was the right consistency. Then she lifted the pink baby into the pink highchair and the yellow baby into the yellow highchair.

"Yuck!" Caroline said. "They're wet again. I just changed them!"

"Yeah," Poochie said matter-of-factly. "They're always wet."

The babies began to bang the trays of their high-chairs with their fists. Caroline used the pink spoon to put oatmeal from the pink bowl into the mouth of the pink twin. Then she switched over and used the yellow spoon to put oatmeal from the yellow bowl into the mouth of the yellow twin. When she looked back at the first highchair, she saw that there was oatmeal in the baby's sparse dark hair.

"Hey!" she said. "How did that happen? I put it into her mouth and now it's in her hair!"

Poochie glanced over. "You have to hold their hands while you feed them," he told her. "Or else they grab it out of their mouths and smear it around." He looked back at the cartoon on TV.

He was right. The second baby, the yellow one, was happily smearing oatmeal into her hair, too.

Caroline filled the pink spoon with oatmeal, moved in toward the pink highchair, and grabbed both of Holly's arms with her left hand. When she had the baby restrained, she poked the oatmeal into the mouth. Holly grinned, gummed the oatmeal, and swallowed. Then Caroline did the same thing with Ivy.

"I think I'm getting the hang of it," she said to Poochie.

"Yeah," Poochie replied, without looking away from the TV.

"But I'm going to have to wash their hair," Caroline said. "Your mother didn't show me how."

"Just sit them in the sink," Poochie said, "and spray them with the squirt thing. They really hate it. They scream."

"Great." Caroline sighed and lunged at Holly with another spoonful of oatmeal.

"I couldn't sleep with all the noise in here." J.P. stood in the kitchen doorway, half asleep, wearing his enormous COACH T-shirt and his pajama bottoms. He yawned and looked around.

One baby, Holly, freshly washed, with her hair still damp, wearing a dry diaper and a clean pink jumpsuit, was lying on her back in the playpen, happily drinking a bottle of milk.

Caroline was on the floor, trying to fasten fresh yellow clothes onto a wiggling, squirming, damp, fussing Ivy, who was anxiously reaching for her bottle.

Both highchairs were smeared with oatmeal.

Caroline had oatmeal in her hair.

There was water all over the kitchen floor, from the babies' baths.

Poochie was still staring at the TV. He had turned up the volume to drown the babies' screaming and was sitting on the floor about ten inches from the set, munching on his third bowl of cereal.

"What's for breakfast?" J.P. asked. "If I'm going to coach a stupid baseball team, I need a really big, nourishing breakfast."

Poochie, without moving his eyes away from the TV, shoved the nearly empty box of dry cereal across the rug toward J.P.

Caroline buttoned Ivy's final button, handed her

the bottle of milk, and plopped her into the playpen beside her sister. She collapsed onto the couch. "I'm dead," she said. "It's only eight o'clock in the morning, and I'm dead. I am not cut out for motherhood. I don't even *like* those babies."

J.P. peered into the playpen. "They're kind of cute," he said. Then he leaned over farther and wrinkled his nose. "But they smell sort of gross. Do they need their diapers changed?"

Six

CAROLINE LOOKED AT HER WATCH. Eleven a.m. This isn't *fair*, she thought; they only slept for an hour, and soon it will be time for their lunch, and then I'll have to bathe them again because they'll have squash and peas in their hair, and I don't even *like* babies, and I wanted to go to the primate seminar, and when the court said we'd have to go to Des Moines, the court probably didn't know about "The Holly and the Ivy"—

Whoops. She'd almost tied a yellow sunbonnet around the head of the pink baby. She switched the little cotton hats, got them on the correct babies, and then lugged them one by one—they were *heavy*—outside to the wide carriage.

The babies sat side by side, smiling and drooling. Carefully Caroline buckled the straps that held them in. She didn't *like* them, but she wasn't going to run the risk of dumping them on the sidewalk.

She pushed the carriage along the wide tree-shaded sidewalk, toward the park where J.P. was coaching the Tater Chips. Again she noticed how different it was from New York. Every house was nicely painted, every yard was neatly mowed, every car looked clean. There were no taxi drivers yelling obscenities at each other the way there were at home. No drunks lying in doorways. No trash littering the sidewalks.

This looked like—well, it looked like *Leave It to Beaver*'s neighborhood. She almost expected Eddie Haskell to come through one of the front doors and say "Good morning" in his wonderfully fake Eddie Haskell voice.

"Gee whiz! Gosh! Golly, hi, Eddie!" Caroline

said aloud, in her Beaver Cleaver voice, and the twins chortled.

As she approached the ball field, she could hear shouts. Even the babies heard the noise. They turned their heads, wide-eyed, listening.

It was hard, at first, to see the ball team itself because of the dust rising around them. Caroline could see heads wearing blue baseball caps, but below the heads was nothing but swirling, tan dust. Out of the dust cloud came the shouts.

She didn't try to get any closer. If she walked the babies into all that dust, she'd have to give them extra baths for *sure*.

"J.P.!" she called. "It's Caroline! It's almost time to come home for lunch!"

The tallest head emerged from the swirling dust, and attached to the head was J.P.'s lanky body in its oversized COACH shirt.

"I said cut it out!" he yelled into the whirlwind of dust. Then he walked over to where Caroline waited with the carriage. He was filthy: sweaty, dusty, with his sneakers untied. Caroline had never seen her brother so disheveled before. In New York, J.P. always wore a tie and jacket to Computer Club.

"What's going on?" Caroline asked, peering beyond J.P. to the mass of yelling little baseball players.

J.P. scowled. "They're fighting," he said. "What time did practice start? Nine o'clock? They've been fighting since nine oh eight."

"Why?"

His shoulders slumped. "I don't know. I told one to practice batting, and he struck out, so he got mad at the pitcher. Another one was supposed to practice throwing, but he threw it the wrong way and hit the third baseman—or maybe I should say third baseperson, since it's a girl—so the third baseman, excuse me, I mean baseperson, punched him in the nose. Then the shortstop started to cry because he missed an infield fly, and two other kids laughed at him for crying, so they all started to fight. It's been that way all morning."

"Well, you're supposed to keep things in order, J.P. That's what a coach is for," Caroline pointed out.

J.P. gave her a long, disdainful look. Then he

leaned over the carriage. "Hi, babies," he said, and tickled Ivy under the chin. "You guys don't fight, do you?" The twins giggled and waved their arms.

"Keep an eye on the babies for a minute, J.P.," Caroline said. She left him there with the carriage and walked over to the screaming mob of little ball-players.

"POOCHIE!" she yelled.

Out of the mass emerged Poochie. His Tater Chips shirt was torn, and he was crying.

"You're a mess, Pooch," Caroline said. "Straighten up. Dry your eyes." Poochie obeyed, wiping his eyes and his running nose on his arm.

"Now tell me some of their names," she said.

"Jason," Poochie sniffled.

"JASON!" roared Caroline. "Stand over here!"

A drippy-nosed redhead emerged from the fight and stood where she indicated.

"Another name, Pooch."

"Adam."

"ADAM!" bellowed Caroline. "Front and center!"

Another scowling Tater Chip emerged from the dusty throng.

"Now Kristin," muttered Poochie.

"KRISTIN!" In a very few minutes, the dust had settled and Caroline was facing a sulking line of twelve six-year-olds. They were all sniffling. They sounded like a Dristan commercial. One little boy had a bloody nose, but it seemed to be subsiding. Two had torn their Tater Chips shirts, but not beyond repair.

"Now," said Caroline—actually, she didn't say it; she *barked* it as if she were a drill sergeant—"what's going on here, people?"

"Kristin hit me with a line drive!" someone called accusingly.

"Eric cheated!" someone else yelled. "Eric is a big poophead!"

"HOLD IT!" Caroline announced. "Shut up, everybody, and listen to me. You guys have to learn to follow orders. Do you know what ORDERS are?"

They all stared at her sullenly. Noses dripped.

"Orders," Caroline went on, "are rules. RULES. Got that?"

Twelve heads nodded.

"And rules have to be obeyed. If you want to play

ball, you have to obey the rules. Do you want to have a good ball team?"

"Yeah," someone muttered.

"I can't hear you," Caroline bellowed. "Do you want the Tater Chips to be a championship ball team?"

"YEAH!" the team members all yelled.

Caroline grinned. "You should try out for the Mormon Tabernacle Choir," she said. "Okay, men. And women. Tie your shoes. Wipe your noses. Be here tomorrow at nine o'clock sharp. DISMISSED!"

Poochie walked beside her as she went back to the baby carriage. J.P. was leaning over, playing with the twins. "They need to be changed," he said, looking up, "and I think they're getting hungry. Do you know what you're supposed to give them for lunch?"

"Of course I do," Caroline told him. She sighed and took the handle of the carriage. They started toward their father's house.

"I can't stand that ball team," J.P. whispered, so that Poochie wouldn't hear.

"And I can't stand these babies," Caroline whispered back.

"You and I, Caroline, we really got stuck. You know what we ought to do?"

"What?" Caroline asked.

Her brother kicked a stone and glanced back at Poochie, who had lagged behind and was walking lopsided, with one foot on the sidewalk and one foot in the street. J.P. looked around to make sure no one was listening. Then he said, "We ought to think up a revenge."

Seven

"Hi there! Boy, am I exhausted! How was your day?"
Lillian Tate asked as she came in from the driveway
and put down her briefcase.

She sounds exactly like Mom, Caroline thought.
"It was okay," she told Lillian.

J.P. didn't say anything.

Poochie grunted without taking his eyes away
from the television. He was sprawled on the floor in
front of the set.

In their playpen, the babies gurgled and kicked.
They had just woken from their afternoon nap and

had had their diapers changed. Now they were each happily chomping with their two teeth on special baby cookies. Caroline could see that already they had gluey cookie crumbs stuck to the creases in their fat little necks. They were going to need baths again before they went to bed.

Why on earth would anybody voluntarily have babies? Caroline wondered. It's just a lot of work and mess.

Lillian went over to the playpen, leaned in, and made kissing noises at the twins. "Hi, Holly," she cooed. "Hi, Ivy. Did you girls have a nice day?"

The twins answered her: gurgle, slobber, spit, burp giggle.

Next Lillian went to the place where Poochie was curled up like a pretzel on the floor, watching cartoons. She kissed the top of his head. "Don't sit so close, Pooch," she said. "How was baseball?"

He wiggled away from her. "I stink at baseball," he muttered.

"J.P. will help you to get better," his mother said cheerfully. "That's what a coach is for." She went to the kitchen and began getting some things out of the refrigerator. Good, thought Caroline; Lillian's going to cook dinner. At least I don't have to do that, too.

"Look who's coming!" Lillian exclaimed, looking through the kitchen window toward the driveway. "Make a date with—" She waited expectantly.

"Herbie Tate," Caroline and J.P. said in unison. Poochie reached forward and turned the sound up a little louder on the TV.

"Ta-DA!" said Herbie Tate as he entered the house. He set a package down, kissed Lillian on the cheek, formed his right hand into a phony gun, and aimed it at Poochie. "Blam," he said. Poochie clutched his stomach, crossed his eyes, and fell over on the carpet, pretending to be dead. "You got me," Poochie said. Then he sat back up and turned his attention to the two cartoon mice who were being chased by a cat.

Herbie leaned over the playpen. "Hi hooooo," he said in a high voice to the babies, who grinned.

Caroline and J.P. stared at each other. Caroline had often fantasized about how nice it would be to have a father at home, instead of just a mother. In her daydreams, the father came in from the office in the evening, wearing a three-piece gray suit, carrying a briefcase and a newspaper. Her daydream father was very intellectual: a professor, or a physicist. He always came home and said, "Good evening," to the family in a deep voice. Maybe he would comment on a world event.

But here, in real life, was her actual father. He was wearing a plaid shirt. He had come home from work, and now he had been in the house for several minutes, and all he had said was . . . Ta-DA. Blam. Hi hooooo.

Now, turning to Caroline and J.P., Herbie stepped back, held his arms away from his sides for a moment, and then suddenly drew two imaginary pistols from two holsters.

"Blam! Blam!" he said, and shot both guns.

Caroline and J.P. didn't move. Poochie glanced up to see if they were doing death scenes. Then he looked back at the TV. Lillian wasn't paying any attention; she was washing some lettuce. Apparently she was used to this.

"Missed," announced Herbie. He blew imaginary

smoke from each imaginary gun and replaced them in their imaginary holsters.

He didn't seem to mind that they hadn't been shot. He picked up the package he had brought home, said, "Think fast!" and tossed it to J.P. J.P. grabbed, startled, but missed. The package landed on the rug.

"It's a present for my Tater Chips coach," Herbie said.

J.P. picked it up and opened it. "Thanks," he said, and turned the baseball glove over and over in his hands.

"Lookee here," Herbie said. He took a small can out of his pocket. "Neatsfoot oil. We rub the glove good, then fold it over and set it under something heavy overnight. A piece of furniture or something. Then in the morning you've got your glove all shaped, ready for use. Pretty soon you'll have a nice pocket in there, just like a major-leaguer. What's your team, J.P.?"

J.P. looked confused. Caroline knew what Herbie meant, but she knew, also, that J.P. didn't. J.P.

didn't follow baseball. He followed chess championships and computer developments.

"Red Sox," Caroline said loudly, to make up for J.P.'s silence.

"Right," said Herbie, apparently pleased with that answer. "After dinner, we'll fix that old glove up for you, just like Jim Rice."

"Gee, great, Dad," J.P. said. Caroline recognized an Eddie Haskell voice.

"Game against the Half-Pints on Friday," Herbie announced. "Are the Chips going to be ready?"

"Half-Pints?" J.P. repeated.

Herbie chuckled. "That's Fred Larrabee's team. He owns a dairy, see, so his team's the Half-Pints. Mine's the Tater Chips—well, you can see why. Then there's Phil Stevenson's team, the Squirts. Guess why they're the Squirts!"

Caroline and J.P. stared at Herbie. They shook their heads.

"Phil manufactures plastic products. His biggest seller: garden hoses. Get it? Squirt!" Herbie aimed an imaginary garden hose toward Caroline and J.P.

"Caroline?" Lillian said from the kitchen.

"Could you put the twins into their highchairs? I have their supper ready. You can feed them while I finish cooking."

"I'll help you, Caroline," J.P. said. "I'll feed the yellow one while you feed the pink one." He laid the baseball glove down on a chair. "Gee, thanks, Dad," he said, Haskell-like, to Herbie. "That was really nice of you."

Herbie smiled broadly. He settled himself on the couch. "How's it going, Poocheroni? Get a hit today? Maybe a home run?"

Poochie shook his head morosely and concentrated on the cartoons.

Caroline and J.P. sat together on Poochie's bed. Poochie was in the bathroom, having his bath. The twins were asleep in their cribs, so Caroline's room was off-limits. There was no place in the house where they could have any privacy, and no time: just these few minutes, huddled together on the bottom bunk, before Poochie's bedtime.

She looked around the little bedroom. The wallpaper appeared to be plaid, at first; but Caroline realized, looking more closely, that the plaid was made up of football goalposts and basketball hoops. The curtains were dark blue, with a little border of red and white football helmets. The bedspreads matched the curtains, with the addition of a huge brown appliqued football in the center of each one.

"I can't stand it," J.P. was muttering.

"It's not that bad," Caroline said, looking around again. "It's bad, but not *that* bad. If you don't look too carefully, you can't tell that the wallpaper is goalposts. And most of the time you're asleep when you're in here, anyway."

J.P. glared at her. "I didn't mean the room, stupid. I mean the whole situation. The whole summer. I can't stand it. I have to run away."

"Don't be a jerk, J.P. You can't run away. Mom would freak out, and there would be lawyers and everything," Caroline pointed out.

"But I can't stand it," J.P. said one more time. He put his head into his hands. "I haven't even been able to open my case of stuff. I won't be able to work on any of my electronics stuff all summer. There's no room and no time. And *now* look. I won't even be able to sleep tonight. I'll be off-balance all night long. My metabolism's going to get all messed up."

He pointed. His newly oiled baseball glove, folded over onto itself, had been placed under one of the legs of the double-decker bed. It was quite thick. The bed tilted noticeably. "Herbie says we won't even feel it," J.P. went on, "but that just proves that Herbie doesn't know me at *all*. I have to be absolutely horizontal when I sleep."

"We could switch beds, just for tonight," Caroline suggested. "I don't mind being tilted when I'm sleeping. But if we switch beds, you'll be in with those disgusting babies. And they'll wake you up at dawn. They'll reach out of their cribs and pull your hair."

"Caroline," J.P. said slowly, "we have to do something. This situation is unbearable."

The splashing in the bathroom had stopped, so they knew that Poochie would be appearing soon, ready for bed. "J.P.," Caroline whispered, "I've been thinking all afternoon. And I have an idea about what I'm going to do. At least I *think* I'm going to. But I have to get my nerve up. It's really a horrible, horrible, horrible revenge."

"What is it?" J.P. asked.

"I can't tell you," Caroline said.

"What do you *mean,* you can't tell me?"

"It's too horrible."

J.P. glared at her angrily. But Poochie opened the door and came in. He was wearing pajamas printed with baseball bats, and there was toothpaste on his chin. He stood there shyly. Finally he said in a low voice, "I been thinking, J.P., that if I sleep on top of the baseball glove, all crooked like that, maybe it will rub off on me and make me a good baseball player."

J.P. didn't say anything.

"Maybe tomorrow I'll get a hit," Poochie said wistfully. He climbed into the lower bunk after Caroline and J.P. stood up.

"Well," J.P. said finally, "maybe."

They turned off Poochie's light and left the room. J.P. muttered as they went down the hall, "If that's the way you feel, I'm not going to tell you what I've been dreaming up, either. I bet mine's more horrible than yours."

"It couldn't be," Caroline replied. "It couldn't possibly."

EIGHT

CAROLINE LAY AWAKE THAT NIGHT, in her bed between the babies' cribs. J.P. had decided to sleep in his lopsided bed after all. He was mad at Caroline because she wouldn't tell him her plan. The Tate Détente, he said, was called off. He had seceded from the United Tates.

But she couldn't tell him. She couldn't tell anyone, not even J.P. It really was too horrible. She lay there staring at the ceiling and thinking of the revenge she had figured out. It was the worst thing she had ever done in her life, she was quite sure. And Caroline had done some pretty terrible things in eleven years.

Once, when she was eight, she remembered, there had been some asparagus in the refrigerator. Fresh asparagus. Her mother had paid a fortune for it, and her mother couldn't afford a fortune—but it was spring, and the asparagus at the market down the street was brand-new, bright green—and her mother had bought it for a treat.

The trouble was, Caroline hated asparagus more than anything in the world. At least when she was eight (Later, when she was nine, it was broccoli. Ten, beets. And eleven, eggplant.)

So when her mother was at work—and the asparagus was going to be cooked for dinner that night—Caroline removed it from the refrigerator and flushed it all down the toilet. One stalk at a time. It took twenty flushes, and at the end of it the toilet sounded totally exhausted, as if *it* hated asparagus, too.

She had never confessed, either. With a perfectly

wide-eyed, honest look, she had told her mother that a burglar had apparently broken into the apartment and stolen the asparagus.

That was a pretty horrible thing to do, Caroline thought, lying in her bed in Des Moines.

Then she remembered something more recent and worse than the asparagus. Just this past spring, when her mother had been dating the professor from Columbia who lived upstairs, Caroline and J.P. had decided that he was a murderer, and they were going to have him put in jail. They had broken into his apartment, looking for evidence, and—

Well. That was almost too horrible to think about.

But this, she realized, tossing restlessly in her bed, was worse. And she was going to do it. She was going to do it soon.

In the next room, in the top bunk, with Poochie below him snoring a little, J.P. also stared at the ceiling. He was really mad at Caroline because she wouldn't tell him her revenge. But he could understand why. Because now that he had dreamed up one, too, he realized that some things are just too horrible to tell.

Whatever Caroline had thought up, J.P. mused, his was worse. He was quite sure. His was unspeakably horrible.

One thing about summer in Des Moines, Caroline thought as she watched baseball practice the next morning: the weather's always good. Her shirt was sticking to her in the heat, and she wished that she had a bonnet, the way the twins did, to shade her eyes.

"Catch it, Pooch! Catch it!" Caroline yelled from where she stood with the baby carriage, at the edge of the ball field.

Poochie had both hands, the left one with a huge baseball glove on it, up in the air. The ball came sailing toward him. It wasn't a fast ball. It was a slow, lazy fly ball that had been hit by Matthew Birnbaum, the only kid on the Tater Chips team who could hit.

Poochie squinted in the sun, ducked as the ball

came closer, and reached up awkwardly. The ball fell between his outstretched arms to the ground and rolled toward second base. The second baseman, Christopher McGowan, dived for it, tripped on an untied shoelace, and fell. He burst into tears and rubbed his scraped chin.

The ball rolled a little farther and came to rest near the pitcher's mound. J.P. picked it up.

"That's enough batting practice, I guess," he called in a resigned voice. He took his notebook out of his back pocket. "Okay, let's see how we did today. Gather around."

The twelve Tater Chips came to stand in a circle around their coach. Caroline pushed the baby carriage across the field and got closer so she could hear what he was saying to them.

"How many people got a hit today?" J.P. asked, with his pencil ready to write it down. Matthew Birnbaum raised his hand. "I got ten hits," he called.

"I sort of got a hit," said the little bucktoothed boy named Eric.

"Anybody else?" asked J.P. Ten ballplayers shook their heads miserably.

"How about catches?" J.P. asked. "Who caught a fly ball today?"

"Me! Me! Me!" All the team members raised their hands eagerly.

"It doesn't count if you *dropped* it," J.P. pointed out.

All of the hands went down. Eric, the little boy who looked like a beaver, raised his hand again, tentatively. J.P. looked at him suspiciously. "Eric?" he said. "I don't remember you catching a fly ball today."

Eric nodded vigorously. "Yeah, I was out there by third base, remember? And I caught it barehanded! You saw me!"

J.P. stared at him. "But, Eric, that was a ball that you threw into the air yourself. Then you caught it when it came back down."

Eric nodded again. "Yeah! Right! I caught it!"

"Poophead Eric! Poophead Eric!" yelled another boy. "You can't catch!"

"Quiet!" J.P. bellowed. He made a checkmark in his notebook. "Anybody get any grounders on the first hop?" he asked.

No one raised a hand. "I would have," Matthew Birnbaum said, "but stupid Kristin got in my way."

"I did not!" shouted Kristin. "You dumb bomb-brain Birnbaum!"

Caroline backed the baby carriage away from the dust cloud that rose as the scuffle began. Holly and Ivy peered over the edge of the carriage, their eyes wide, at the sound of angry shouts.

Finally the fight subsided. Several Tater Chips were crying and, as usual, one had a bloody nose, and several shirts were ripped. "See you tomorrow at practice," J.P. said as he walked away, Poochie trudging behind. "Don't forget we have the big game against the Half-Pints on Friday. That's just three days away!

"I wonder what their mothers think when they come home," he said to Caroline. "They always look as if they've been in a war."

"They *have* been," Caroline pointed out. She tilted the carriage to get it up over the curb as they crossed the street. The babies slipped forward, and the one in the pink hat started to whimper. "You ought to help them more, J.P. *Teach* them how to hit and throw and catch. They're just little kids, for heaven's sake. Shhh, Holly. Quit crying." She jiggled the carriage. But the baby in the yellow hat joined her sister and they both began to wail.

"Quit criticizing, Caroline," J.P. said. "What do you know about it? You don't have any idea what it's like, to get stuck with a job you don't want and don't know how to do. And quit shaking the carriage. No *wonder* they're crying. Here, give it to me."

J.P. took the handle of the baby carriage. He stopped it, leaned in, and spoke to the babies. "Hey, girls. Shhhh. No problem; you just slid forward. Here. I'll put you back where you belong." One by one he lifted the babies back against their pillows and settled them there. Holly's crying stopped; her chin quivered, and she smiled, finally, up at J.P. Then Ivy stopped wailing abruptly and grinned. J.P. pushed the carriage forward, ignoring Caroline.

She didn't care. She had turned back to walk with Poochie, who was plodding along unhappily, rubbing his eyes with his arm and sniffling.

"Of course you can learn to hit, Pooch," she was

telling him. "This afternoon I'll work with you out in the back yard. We'll practice keeping your eye on the ball, okay?"

"Okay," Poochie sniffled. "But don't throw them hard. J.P. always throws them wicked hard."

"I won't," Caroline reassured him. "We'll start real slow. Now: no more crying."

"Okay." Poochie gave one last moist sniffle and grinned up at her.

"Shoulders straight," Caroline said.

He pulled his little slumped shoulders upright and took a deep breath. "Okay," he said.

In the afternoon while the babies slept, Caroline worked with Poochie in the yard for more than an hour. At the end of that time, she flopped, exhausted, into the grass. Poochie sank down beside her eagerly.

"I'm better now, aren't I?" he asked. "I'm better! I know I'm better!"

Caroline put her arm around him and nodded. "You sure are, Pooch. You really got some hits!"

She had been keeping count in her head. Her

arm ached from pitching to Poochie: slow, accurate pitches that almost contacted the bat on their own. She had counted each one.

One hundred and fourteen. She had pitched one hundred and fourteen pitches.

And he had hit four of them. Caroline wasn't a math genius like J.P., so she didn't know how to figure out Poochie's batting average. But he had hit four out of one hundred and fourteen, and it was bound to be a big improvement over his previous batting average, which had been zero.

NINE

ONE THING CAROLINE HAD TO ADMIT: Dinner was better in Des Moines than it was in New York.

It wasn't that Caroline's mother was a bad cook. Actually, she was a pretty good cook, and she had a collection of recipes that she tore out of magazines in the laundromat and the dentist's office. The trouble was, she never had much time for cooking. She didn't get home from her job at the bank until five thirty every evening, and she was always exhausted by then.

And she didn't have much money for groceries. Sometimes, in the supermarket, she would pick up a package of chicken breasts and look at it longingly for a minute. But then she would say, "I just can't afford two ninety-nine a pound for chicken breasts, Caroline." Caroline would nod understandingly, and her mother would put the chicken breasts back. She would reach for the chicken *livers,* which cost ninety-nine cents a pound. Caroline would sigh and plan to eat a peanut butter sandwich for dinner.

Now, in Des Moines, right before her very eyes as she fed the babies their supper, Caroline watched Lillian take two packages of chicken breasts out of the refrigerator and unwrap them.

"What do you think, Caroline?" Lillian asked. "Shall we grill these outside tonight? I could make a barbecue sauce."

Caroline nodded appreciatively as she spooned some of a disgusting apricot and tapioca mixture into Ivy's mouth.

Ivy stuck out her tongue, made a sound that was

something like "Bpheeewwww," and grinned as the apricots and tapioca flew into the air toward Caroline.

J.P. looked up from his notebook, where he was working on the baseball team statistics. "I taught her to do that," he said, "while you were out in the yard with Poochie this afternoon. The twins woke up from their naps, and I went in and played with them for a while. I was trying to teach them to whistle."

"Thanks a *lot*," Caroline said sarcastically as she wiped the apricots and tapioca off her own face.

"She couldn't get the hang of it," J.P. explained. "She can only do that 'Bpheeewwww.'"

"You have to have top teeth to whistle," Poochie announced, looking up from the TV cartoons. "They don't have any top teeth."

"*Wrong*," said J.P. "That's what I thought, too. So I was conducting this experiment. And look." He stood up and came over to the highchairs.

Caroline spooned some apricots and tapioca into Holly, and held her hands firmly so that she wouldn't smear the food on her face.

"Hey, Holl," J.P. said, leaning over the highchair. "Give a little whistle." He whistled at her, and then stood back.

Holly puckered up and whistled. A splat of apricots and tapioca landed on Caroline's shoulder.

"See?" said J.P. "Holly can whistle. But Ivy can't. And they both have the same teeth—just on the bottom—so it isn't the teeth. I'm trying to figure out what makes the difference."

"Bpheeewwww," said Ivy, and more food flew.

"*Here*," said Caroline angrily, and handed her brother both bowls of baby food. "You find them so fascinating—you feed them."

The chicken breasts were terrific. The family ate outside on the picnic table in the yard, and there were more than enough barbecued chicken breasts to go around; and there was a mountain of salad, with blue cheese dressing—Caroline's favorite—and there was strawberry ice cream for dessert.

The babies' playpen had been moved outside, and Holly and Ivy gurgled and kicked happily.

"Can I practice batting again, before I have my

bath?" Poochie asked, with his mouth full of ice cream.

"Sure, fella," Herbie Tate boomed. "Coach here'll hold a little BP after dinner, won'tcha, Coach?" He thumped J.P. on the shoulder.

J.P. winced. "BP?" he asked, looking puzzled.

"Batting practice," Caroline translated. Sometimes J.P., for all his IQ, was so *thick*.

Her brother groaned. "Do I have to?"

"I'll do it," Caroline suggested. "I was helping Poochie this afternoon," she explained to her father.

Herbie Tate was swinging an imaginary baseball bat and hitting imaginary home runs over the roof of the garage. He wasn't paying any attention to anything else. "Gotta go," he said after he had watched the final invisible ball disappear into a neighbor's tree. "Gotta lot of paperwork to do down at the store."

He kissed Lillian. "Great dinner, Diamond Lil," he said.

He shot each baby with his imaginary pistols. "Blam. Blam. Love ya," he said. They giggled and waved their arms.

Then he took on a boxing stance, did some quick shuffling with his feet, and aimed some fake punches at Poochie, who was still shoveling ice cream into his mouth. "Go for it, Champ," he said. Poochie put his spoon down and gave him a halfhearted left jab into the air. "Right, Daddy," he said.

Herbie turned toward Caroline and J.P.

"Good night, Dad," they both said quickly in unison, like the Mormon Tabernacle Choir.

"Thank you for taking over the batting practice," J.P. said to Caroline. They were out in the yard, sitting by the picnic table, slapping at occasional mosquitoes and watching the coals in the charcoal grill turn white. The babies were in bed, and so was Poochie. Lillian was washing her hair, and Herbie hadn't come back yet from the sporting goods store.

"You're welcome," Caroline told her brother. "I don't mind, ah, BP." She giggled. "Actually," she said, "Poochie's getting better. I think I figured out what his problem—"

J.P. interrupted her. "I don't *care* what his

problem is. *My* problem is that I'm not going to survive this summer, Caroline. I may not survive this *week*. Not with that big baseball game on Friday. Caroline, I hate baseball more than anything in the whole world. You remember in that book, Caroline, and then they made a movie of it — *1984* — they chose a special torture for everyone. The guy in the book, his torture was rats, remember? Because he hated rats more than anything in the world. But me, Caroline, *my* special torture would be — my special torture *is* —"

"Baseball."

"Right," groaned J.P. "Baseball."

"Mine is babies," muttered Caroline.

"I think those babies are cute," J.P. said.

Caroline took a long deep breath. "Maybe I'm an unnatural person," she said, "but I think those babies are about as cute as — as cute as —" She paused, trying to think of her least favorite thing in the whole world.

"Tarantulas?" J.P. suggested, trying to be helpful.

Caroline glared at him. "J.P.," she said in her

paleontologist's voice, "tarantulas are actually very fascinating creatures. I would *much* rather have a pet tarantula than a baby."

"Well, *I'd* rather have a baby than a baseball team," J.P. replied gloomily.

They were both silent for a moment. Then they heard the car approach, turn into the driveway, and pull to a stop. They heard the car door open and close. They heard their father's booming voice as he headed for the kitchen door.

"Ta-DA!" called Herbie Tate. "Here he is, folks: the Indestructible, Late, Great, Herbieeeeee TATE!"

They heard Lillian greet him, laughing.

"I'm going to do my revenge tomorrow," whispered Caroline to her brother.

J.P. gave a sudden, sinister laugh. "Guess what," he said. "I already did mine."

TEN

CAROLINE JUMPED, STARTLED, when she heard the footsteps coming toward the back door. She looked at her watch — only 10:30. Too early for J.P.'s baseball practice to end.

The babies were still asleep.

Lillian was at her real estate course.

And Caroline was feeling guilty, because that morning, alone in the house — except, of course, for Holly and Ivy — she had performed her act of revenge.

Now it was done. It could never be undone, even if she wanted to undo it, which she didn't.

But she felt guilty. And there *were*—she listened more carefully—footsteps coming toward the back door.

The police? The police couldn't *possibly* know what she had done.

Caroline crept nervously over to the kitchen window. She peered out, laughed in relief, and went *to* the door.

"Hi," she said to her father.

Herbie Tate looked surprised to see her. His shoulders were slumped, the way Poochie's were sometimes. He appeared a little confused and finally began to reach halfheartedly for the imaginary pistol with which he usually greeted them. Then he sighed and didn't bother.

"Hi, Caroline," he said. "I forgot you'd be here. Stupid of me."

"The babies are asleep," Caroline explained. "After they wake up I'll walk them down to the park where J.P. and Poochie are practicing."

Her father slumped onto the couch in the family

room and shook his head. "Of course. I forgot. Lil's off at that real estate thing. Poor Lil."

"Why 'Poor Lil'?" Caroline asked a little defensively. "She's got a great babysitter—cheap, I might add."

Her father stared at her. "We haven't thanked you enough, Caroline. I'm sorry. I guess I ought to explain. I said 'Poor Lil' because she hates that real estate course. She doesn't want to be a real estate agent. Lil would rather stay home and be a mother than anything else in the world."

"Well, why doesn't she? Why on earth would someone become a real estate agent if she didn't want to?" Caroline asked, confused.

Herbie shrugged. He looked embarrassed. "Money," he said finally. "Things aren't so good down at the store, Caroline."

"But I thought—"

He shook his head. "It's only temporary. A temporary slump. Don't tell Poochie. Please don't tell Poochie."

Tell Poochie? Why on earth would she tell a six-year-old kid that his father was having financial problems? And speaking of Poochie, Caroline thought—

"Does he have a *name*, Dad? A real name? Something that isn't Poochie?"

Her father smiled. "Of course he does. David Herbert Tate."

"Then *why*—"

"After Lillian and I got married, I wanted a kid right away. Because I missed you guys, Caroline. I missed you and J.P. It was really fun having you around when you were little. Your mom and I didn't have a very good marriage, but we sure both liked you kids a lot."

"Well, if you missed us so much, you could have made us come for the summer," Caroline pointed out.

"I know," her father said. "But—well, maybe you won't understand this, Caroline. But I wanted my very own full-time kid again."

"So you had one, and you named him—"

"Wait. Hold it. Lillian didn't want to have a child right away. She wasn't sure she'd be a good mother.

We had a big argument. I wanted a kid. She wanted a dog."

"And you won."

Herbie chuckled. "I won. And Lillian turned out to be the best mother around. But for a little joke—well, we named him David Herbert. But we've always called him Pooch."

"Oh." Caroline squirmed. Pooch was a disgusting nickname, she thought. But she didn't want to tell her father that.

"Anyway," her father went on, "like I said, I'd appreciate it if you wouldn't mention what I told you to Poochie."

"I wouldn't do that, Dad."

"Because he has his big game coming up and all. Don't want to distract him, right?" Herbie Tate stood up. Caroline could almost see him putting his other personality back on, as if he were putting on a coat. "Gotta get back to the old store. I just came home to pick up some ledgers from the study. The ole federal marshal's comin' into town on his horse, to check over my books."

He moved heavily down the hall toward the study, and after a moment he came back with a handful of papers and a briefcase. He sorted through the papers, stacked them, and put them into the briefcase. He sighed.

"This will all get cleared up," he said. "This will all be cleared up real soon. I'm sure of it." He turned the briefcase over and over in his hands. Caroline watched him.

"Dad," she said, "you're really worried, aren't you? You're talking about *big* trouble, aren't you?"

He nodded and was silent for a moment. Then he said in a puzzled voice, "I really can't understand it. The store's always been successful. Okay, so maybe a sporting goods store isn't impressive like a huge corporation—so it's not IBM or GE. But it's always been a good store, Caroline. People in Des Moines have always come to Tate's Sporting Goods for their tennis rackets, for their golf clubs—"

He shook his head and stared out the window. "I've just never had any problems. A couple of months ago I had to fire someone because I caught him stealing some things. That was the biggest problem I've ever had at work." Herbie laughed sadly. "Big deal. I had to let the fellow who ran the computer go, because he took two tennis rackets. We didn't even prosecute.

"But I guess that was just the start of a run of bad luck. It's been a nightmare since then. I thought we were making plenty of money—we've always made plenty of money this time of year—but the money isn't there.

"I don't know where it went. And I'm in charge—it's my responsibility—it's my store. Meet your fate with Herbie Tate, right?"

He stood up with a rueful smile. "Back to the salt mines. I have three accountants in there trying to sort things out. And they're costing me seventy-five dollars an hour. Apiece."

Slowly he took out his imaginary pistol. This time he aimed it at his own head. "Blam," he said. Then he added quickly, with a nervous laugh, "Only joking."

Caroline watched through the window as he backed the car out of the driveway. Her throat hurt. He should have explained before, she thought. I wouldn't have minded babysitting. I would have come to Des Moines to help out, without even complaining, if I had known.

And I sure wouldn't have done what I did this morning, she thought, feeling a little like crying. Because I can't undo it.

Through the closed bedroom door, down the hall, she heard the little thumping and laughing sounds as the babies began to wake up.

Caroline arrived at the ball field with the babies in their carriage at the usual time, just as practice was about to end.

Out in center field, Matthew Birnbaum was industriously picking his nose. In right field, Eric the Beaver was hopping up and down, in circles, as if he were practicing ballet. Someone unidentifiable was lying on his — or maybe *her* — back in left field, getting a suntan.

Poochie was at bat, and J.P. was throwing to him.

"Pooch!" Caroline called. "Don't forget to —"

J.P. glared at her. "Do you mind?" he asked sarcastically.

"Well, I was practicing with him yesterday, remember?" Caroline called. "And I realized—"

"You want to take over as coach?" J.P. yelled angrily.

Yes, Caroline thought. I'd love to. And I could do a better job of it, too. But she didn't say that. "I'm sorry," she called to her brother. "I'll wait for you over by the bleachers. I want to talk to you after practice."

She steered the heavy carriage toward the bleachers and parked it so that the babies were in the shade. One of the twins—she peered in and saw that it was the one in the yellow hat—was fretful. She whimpered and pulled at her hat. Her face was flushed.

"Shhh," Caroline said impatiently and jiggled the carriage.

When practice, followed by all the usual after-practice insults, punching, kicking, name-calling, and crying, had ended, J.P. and Caroline walked home with the babies and Poochie. Caroline wanted to tell her brother about her conversation with Herbie. But she had promised not to tell Pooch, and Poochie was walking beside them.

"You know what we were talking about before, J.P.?" Caroline asked. "Something that you were going to do—actually, you already did it—and something that I was going to do?"

J.P. looked at her as if she were speaking a foreign language. She gestured toward Poochie to explain why she was being so secretive. "Yeah," J.P. said finally. "What about it?"

"Well, ah, is yours undoable?"

J.P. considered that. "If I undid it right away, it would be," he said. "But there's a time limit on that. Why?"

"Well," Caroline explained miserably, "I did mine this morning, and there's no way to undo mine. And I wish there were. I'll tell you why later."

"It had better be good," J.P. said. "Because only some gigantic reason would make me undo mine."

"This is truly gigantic," Caroline said emphatically.

Poochie looked up. "Like the Incredible Hulk, I betcha," he said.

"Exactly," Caroline said.

Eleven

"WELL, I DON'T UNDERSTAND THAT *AT ALL*," J.P. said. "How can he be on the verge of bankruptcy? We had steak for dinner the other night. And he gave me that baseball glove. Even though I hate it, it's probably worth forty bucks."

They were sitting privately on the back patio after lunch. The babies were having their naps, and Poochie was, as usual, crouched in front of the TV with his thumb in his mouth.

"I know it sounds weird," Caroline explained, "but I think when you're in HUGE financial trouble, you can still eat steak and chicken breasts. It's *small* financial trouble, like Mom has, when you have to eat hamburger and chicken livers. This is different."

J.P. picked at a splintered corner of the picnic table. "Yeah," he said, "I guess. And I feel bad for him in a way. But it must be his own fault. He must be a bad businessman."

Caroline stretched her legs out in the sunshine. She watched a bird hop from one end of a tree branch to another. She yawned. One of the babies had fussed during the night and woken her up several times. "I feel sorry for him," she said. "He said everything had always been just fine. And then a couple of months ago he had to fire somebody, and that started a whole run of bad luck."

"Why did he have to fire somebody?"

Caroline laughed. "The guy stole two tennis rackets. What a stupid thing to do. He probably made a good salary. It was the guy who ran Dad's computer. Wouldn't you think he could afford to *buy* tennis rackets?"

J.P. sat up straight suddenly. "Dad has a *computer?*"

Caroline shrugged. "That's what he said. What's the big deal about that? Don't most stores have computers these days?"

J.P. looked stricken. "I don't believe it," he groaned. "All this time, he has a computer down at the store, and he didn't even tell me. He's got me coaching this ridiculous baseball team, and I *could* have been down at the store hacking around on his computer. I *could* have been having a decent summer."

Caroline stood up. "I have to do the lunch dishes," she said. "I wish you'd quit feeling so sorry for yourself and start feeling sorry for Dad. You're having a rotten summer, true. But *he's* going to have a rotten *life* if he goes bankrupt."

But J.P. wasn't listening to her. He was slumped over, with his head hanging down and his elbows on his scrawny knees. "He didn't even tell me," he muttered. "I could have been in there all day. I could even have *worked* for him, running the computer. I wouldn't even steal stupid tennis rackets."

He was still muttering as Caroline headed for the house.

"Don't sit so close," she said automatically to Poochie as she passed, and he moved his head a fraction of an inch away from the TV screen.

One of the babies began to wail.

An hour later, Caroline was rocking the baby wearing the yellow sunsuit, trying to get her back into her usual good mood. But she squirmed in Caroline's lap, whimpered, and pulled at her own ear.

"Poochie," Caroline said finally, "please, would you turn off the TV for a while? With the baby crying, it's really driving me crazy. J.P.'s out back. Why don't you see if he'll toss a few balls for batting practice?"

Poochie turned the TV off, stood up, rubbed his eyes, and looked through the window. J.P. was still at the picnic table, staring into space.

Poochie frowned apprehensively. "He looks like he's thinking," he said.

Caroline leaned forward and observed her brother. "Yeah," she agreed. "That's his 'I'm thinking' look. Maybe we'd better not disturb him."

But suddenly, as they watched, J.P. leaped to his

feet. He clapped his hands together. "Obvious!" he said aloud. They could hear him through the open window. "*Totally* obvious!"

He came charging through the kitchen door and let it bang shut behind him. He stood in the middle of the kitchen floor with his arms out and his shoulders straight and his chin up. He looked like Clark Kent immediately after he had changed into Superman.

"Totally, wickedly, completely, *awesomely* OBVIOUS!" J.P. bellowed. "I have to call Dad. What's the phone number of the store, Pooch? I need it instantaneously."

Poochie shrugged. "I dunno. Wait a minute." He went to the refrigerator and took down a brown magnetized potholder shaped like a basketball. "Here," he said and handed it to J.P.

J.P. glanced at the potholder. "'DINNER WILL WAIT,'" he read, "'FOR—'" He looked up expectantly at Poochie and Caroline.

"'HERBIE TATE,'" they both replied.

"Very tasteful," J.P. said with a grimace. "But there's the phone number." He went to the telephone and dialed the number that was printed on the pot-holder.

Caroline gave the fussy baby a cracker and put her into the playpen next to her sister, who was chewing on a toy. She listened with interest to J.P. as he talked on the telephone to Herbie.

"Dad," J.P. was saying, "I can't be positive without coming down there to check it out, but I am almost positive that I know what's gone wrong at the store."

Caroline watched as J.P. listened impatiently to his father's voice.

"No," J.P. said, "Poochie's not listening. He's watching TV. Listen, Dad, if you'd just let me come down and check the computer system—"

There was another impatient silence as J.P. listened. His shoulders were stiff.

"I *know* I'm only thirteen, Dad. But I've been studying computers at school in New York for five years. *Age* doesn't matter; it's how your brain works. My brain works like a computer. I'm a crummy baseball player, Dad, but I'm a *genius* at computers!"

More tense silence as J.P. listened in frustration.

"Dad—"

He sighed and listened some more.

"Dad. I know you have the accountants there, and I know how much they're costing you. But I am almost *sure* that if you'd give me a chance, I could solve the whole thing this afternoon.

"Hey, Dad, how about letting me speak to one of the accountants? Just for a minute, okay?"

J.P. waited. His eyes lit up. He whispered across the room to Caroline, "He's getting the accountant. Maybe I can convince *him*."

He turned back to the telephone. "Sir? This is James P. Tate, Herbie Tate's son. Listen, sir, I'm only thirteen, but I think I know what the problem is at the store. There was an employee who was fired a while back, and he had access to the computer. I think he sabotaged the financial records before he left."

J.P. listened for a moment. "Yessir," he said. "Thirteen. But, sir, I *know* computers. I know how he could have done it. And if he did what I *think* he did, the database still has its integrity. Do you have a BASIC interpreter on the system?"

He sighed and listened. With his hand over the mouthpiece, he whispered to Caroline, "This guy doesn't know anything about computers."

He turned back to the telephone. "Yessir," he said, "I could. I don't want to just kludge something together, though. I want to write a system, a whole new interface with the database, and then we could—"

The man interrupted, and J.P. waited.

"Thank you, sir," he said at last. "I'll be ready."

He hung up. His forehead was sweaty, and he was breathing hard. But he was grinning. "They're sending a car for me," he told his sister.

Caroline and Poochie watched from the doorway as J.P., wearing his enormous COACH shirt, but with his shoulders straight and firm inside it, was motioned over to a dark sedan by two men in business suits. Both of them were talking to J.P. at the same time.

J.P. was nodding professionally as he listened to them.

He interrupted them politely just as they reached the car parked in the driveway. "Of course you could be right," he said. "But I feel fairly certain that what we're going to find is a discrepancy between the database and the report maker. Now, that could be programmed into catalogue sales, or front registers, or both, and—"

He got into the car, then looked back at Caroline and called, "I may be gone all night!"

Caroline nodded and waved. She felt very proud of her brother and very hopeful that her father's problems would be solved.

But Poochie let out a howl. "All night? What about baseball practice? The big game's day after tomorrow!"

Caroline put her arm around him. "I'll take over," she said. "I'll coach."

Twelve

The phone rang late in the evening as Lillian and Caroline sat nervously in the family room pretending to be interested in a rerun of *Charles in Charge*.

"It's for you, Caroline," Lillian said after she had talked for a moment. "It's J.P., and he says everything's turning out just the way he thought it would. Does that mean we're okay? I can't understand any of this."

Caroline nodded happily as she went to the phone in the kitchen. She felt very relieved for Lillian and her father. "I don't understand any of it either," she said. "Not the computer stuff, anyway. But if J.P. says it's all okay, well, then it's all okay. J.P. is a genius."

She picked up the receiver. "Hi, J.P.," she said, laughing. "I hope you didn't hear what I just said to Lillian. It would make you conceited."

"Is Lillian right there?" J.P. asked in a low voice. "I don't want her to hear this conversation."

Caroline glanced into the family room. Lillian had picked up some knitting. Then she cocked her head slightly, listening to something: a wail from the bedroom where the babies were. She put the knitting down and disappeared down the hall to check the twins.

"No," Caroline told her brother. "I'm all alone. Why? I thought everything was okay."

"It is," J.P. said. "But I'm going to be here most of the night, though, unraveling all of this. I want you to take over baseball practice in the morning if you can."

"Sure. I already told Pooch that I would. No sweat. Lillian's going to stay home with the babies. One of them has a fever. And anyway, if things are okay at the store, and Herbie's not bankrupt after all—"

"He isn't," J.P. said. "The money's all there. It was in the database, but the report maker was sabotaged, like I thought."

"Well then. Lillian can quit the real estate course!"

"I want you to sneak into my room," J.P. said. "Don't wake Pooch up. Get my notebook out of my suitcase—it's under some of my electronic stuff."

"Okay. Why?"

"You'll need it for baseball practice. Listen, Caroline—Dad's coming, so I have to say this fast—"

"What?"

J.P. was whispering. "*Undo* it. Everything in the notebook. You'll see when you look at it. Undo my revenge. Tomorrow's the last possible chance.

"I gotta go," he said suddenly. "Good luck."

And J.P. hung up the telephone.

Caroline walked with Poochie to the ball field in the morning. It was very relaxing, not feeding babies and changing babies and bathing babies. Back at the house, Lillian was doing all of that. Even the fussing and feverish baby seemed to notice the difference and was in a better mood now that her mother had taken over.

Caroline flipped through the pages of J.P.'s notebook as she walked.

"Poochie," she said, "I'm going to make some changes this morning, since I'm coaching."

Poochie nodded happily. "Now I'll get some hits," he said. "J.P. didn't know that I—"

Caroline interrupted him. "Things will be different now," she said.

J.P.'s revenge had been truly rotten. But she didn't want Poochie to know about it, ever. At least she was going to undo it. Her own revenge had been not only rotten but was also undoable; and she could only hope that no one would ever find out about it.

She flipped through the pages of the notebook again. As soon as practice was over this morning, she would destroy the incriminating pages. But for now, she needed them.

Each page held a player's name. And then it listed all that player's baseball-playing flaws. She had to give J.P. credit; he wasn't much of an ath-lete or a coach, but he certainly was observant. He had noticed the smallest details of each little player's baseball style. Then he had planned the big game tomorrow to take maximum advantage of every single flaw.

He had programmed the Tater Chips to lose. He couldn't have done it more effectively if he had used a computer.

Turning back to the page marked "Poochie," she realized that J.P. had already noticed the same things that she had. One of Poochie's problems, unfortunately, was not going to be solved by tomorrow's game.

"Pooch," Caroline began to ask, as the baseball field came into view around the corner, "who's that kid waiting there in the bleachers? I can't remember his name." She pointed to Matthew Birnbaum, who was punching his fist into his glove rhythmically as he waited for the team to assemble.

Poochie looked toward the bleachers, where Caroline was pointing. He squinted. "Where?" he asked.

Caroline squatted on the sidewalk beside him so

that her face was level with his. She pointed again, very carefully, to Matthew Birnbaum.

"See that kid in the bleachers?" she asked.

Poochie squinted so hard that his face was distorted. "No," he said finally.

"Do you see the bleachers?" Caroline asked.

"Sort of," Poochie said uncertainly.

Caroline took his hand. Slowly they walked on toward the ball field. "Poochie," she said, "you need glasses. And it will take a little while to get your eyes examined and then to have the glasses made. So they won't be ready for tomorrow's game. But probably by the *next* big game, you'll be able to see."

Poochie squinted up at her in amazement. "You mean when the ball is coming at me, I'll be able to *see* it?"

"Right. After you get glasses."

"Then I'll be able to *catch* it!"

"Right. And hit it, too."

Poochie grinned. "I can already hit it, Caroline. Even when I can't see it, I can hit it sometimes, if I bat lefty."

Caroline nodded. It was amazing, considering

Poochie's terrible eyesight. But he *could* bat. It was just that he was left-handed, and he'd been batting right-handed until Caroline had turned him around. His batting average had skyrocketed immediately from zero to .05.

If Poochie could get an occasional hit when he was blind, imagine what his average would be after he got glasses!

"You might be the star of this team by the end of the summer, Pooch," Caroline said.

Carefully she tore out the page marked "Poochie," so that he would never know what was written on it: "Practically blind. Left-handed. Make him bat right-handed, and he'll never get a hit."

Caroline crumpled the page and tossed it into the trash can at the entrance to the ball field. Then she leaned the notebook against one of the bleacher seats and started a new page. "Poochie," she wrote. "Get Lillian to take him to eye doctor. Be sure he bats left-handed."

She looked at the new page. She crossed out "Poochie." Above it she wrote, "David Herbert Tate."

Then she sighed. She had eleven other pages to

deal with. And when she looked up, she saw that all eleven other players had arrived now and were poking each other and scuffling in the bleachers.

It was going to be a very long morning. She adjusted J.P.'s baseball cap on her head. It was a little too large, and it bent the tops of her ears.

"C'mon, troops!" Caroline called and clapped her hands. "Let's get to work! We gotta make some changes in the way this team operates, because after tomorrow we're going to be—"

"CHAMPIONS!" the twelve little ballplayers shouted as they scrambled down from the bleachers and headed for the field.

Thirteen

The house was quiet for a change. No wailing babies—the twins were asleep. No TV—Poochie had gone to bed, promising to practice batting in his dreams for tomorrow's game. And even J.P. was asleep. He had been up all through the previous night and had wandered around groggily during the day, calling the store occasionally to make sure that the computer was still giving out the correct information. Finally, at seven p.m., he had gone to bed.

Caroline was sitting in the family room with

Lillian and her father. Herbie Tate was going through a stack of papers.

"I can't believe it," he said, looking up. "I can't believe I have a son who is such a genius. Did I tell you what one of the accountants said after he watched J.P. at work on the computer?"

"Yes," Caroline and Lillian said. "You told us several times."

"And did I tell you that our financial situation is just fine, Lillian? The income was all there the whole time. It was just that it was concealed, apparently, by the way the computer had been programmed—"

"Yes," Lillian said, laughing. "You told me, Herbie. The instant you told me, I resigned from the real estate course." She put her knitting down. "How about some iced tea?"

Caroline and Herbie both nodded, and Lillian went to the refrigerator.

Herbie set his papers aside and shook his head. "Revenge," he said. "The guy got fired for stealing two tennis rackets, and he was lucky I didn't prosecute. Imagine doing something like this for revenge. If I had any idea where he is now, I think I'd go after him and—"

Lillian handed him a glass of iced tea. "No you wouldn't, Herb. Because that would be revenge, too."

Caroline took her glass of tea, thanked Lillian, and sipped. She was uncomfortable listening to the talk about revenge. *Very* uncomfortable. But at least J.P.'s revenge had been undone, and the Tater Chips now had a better chance of winning their game tomorrow.

"I know I told you about this, Lillian," Caroline said, "but I want to make sure you don't forget. About Poochie's eyesight—"

"I already made an appointment," Lillian said. "I'm taking him to the ophthalmologist on Monday afternoon. And I'm ashamed of myself that I never realized he needed glasses. I thought *all* kids sat four inches away from the TV."

"He's going to be a really good ballplayer after he gets glasses, Dad," Caroline told Herbie. "Even *without* glasses, I bet anything he gets a hit tomorrow."

Herbie beamed. "I can't wait to watch that game," he said. "Thank goodness the mess is cleared up at the store so I can take the morning off. I'll stop by the store early so that I can pick up your COACH shirt, Caroline, and your cap. Do you need a glove? We wouldn't have time to give it the old neatsfoot oil, but—"

"Nope," Caroline told him. "Thanks anyway. But I really don't need a glove."

Lillian held up the sweater sleeve she was knitting and measured it against one that was already finished. "I'll be late to the game, Caroline," she said. "I wouldn't miss it for anything, but I probably won't get there until the second or third inning. I talked to the pediatrician this afternoon about Ivy's earache, and I'm going to run her over to his office in the morning for a penicillin shot."

"I'll tell Poochie," Caroline said. "His big rooting section will be there by the third inning."

Lillian stood up and went to the refrigerator again. "It won't take long at the doctor's," she said from the kitchen as she poured some more iced tea into her own glass. "It's a good thing it's Ivy, though, who has the earache. Holly's allergic to penicillin."

She brought the pitcher in. "More tea?" she asked Caroline.

Caroline stared at her. "No, thank you," she said finally, in a stricken voice.

"Is something wrong?"

"I'm going to bed," Caroline said tensely. "All of a sudden I feel as if I want to go to bed."

But she couldn't sleep. For hours Caroline lay in the dark bedroom, wide awake. She heard the babies sigh and snore and toss as they slept. After a while she heard Herbie and Lillian go down the hall to their bedroom. She heard the muted sounds of their voices and water running in their bathroom, and then the house was completely silent. And still Caroline couldn't sleep.

Finally she got out of bed. In the bathroom across the hall, she turned on the light, blinked, and looked at her watch. It was after one a.m.

Unhappily she wandered out into the dark family room and sat on the couch. Lillian's partly knitted sweater sleeve was there, on top of the knitting instruction book. Yellow, for Ivy. She had already finished the little pink one for Holly, with a matching cap.

Caroline picked up the little pink cap, turned it over in her hands, and began to cry.

Had she said, just a few days ago, that she hated the babies? It wasn't true. She didn't hate them. It was true that she didn't like taking care of them. She found it boring. And it was true that she hoped *she* would never have twin babies—or maybe any babies—because she would much rather spend her adult life in Asia Minor, digging up fossils and prehistoric skeletons, and she would not have time to knit little sweaters and hats.

But she did *like* Holly and Ivy. And Poochie: *David Herbert Tate*. And Herbie and Lillian, for that matter.

Maybe even *love* would be the right word.

But thinking that made her cry harder. Caroline couldn't come up with any solution to her problem;

there was simply no way to undo what she had already done.

Finally, in desperation, she crept down the dark hall and opened the door to the room that Poochie and J.P. shared.

When her eyes had adjusted to the darkness, she could see that Poochie was sprawled, sound asleep, with his mouth open, on top of his covers. He was wearing his baseball glove.

In the upper bunk, she could see J.P. also, sound asleep with the pillow on top of his head.

Carefully and quietly, Caroline climbed the little ladder to the top bunk. She removed the pillow from her brother's head and whispered, "J.P.?"

"Nnnnnhhhhh."

"J.P.," she repeated a little more loudly. "Wake up. It's Caroline."

"They must be on a LAN," J.P. murmured in his sleep. "I wonder what protocol they were using."

Caroline shook him gently by the shoulder. "J.P.!" she said urgently.

"The jogging shoes database menu is up on one terminal," J.P. said groggily.

"Wake up!" Caroline said aloud. Quickly she glanced down at Poochie, but he was still sound asleep.

J.P. opened his eyes. "Is the tape drive on line?" he asked.

"No," Caroline said, "the sister is on the bunk-bed ladder and about to fall. Wake up, J.P. I need you. Quit dreaming about computers."

J.P. rubbed his eyes. "Whaddaya want?" he asked.

"Shhhhh. Don't wake up Poochie. Meet me out back. I'm in serious trouble." Caroline climbed back down the ladder and tiptoed back across the room and out into the hall. Carefully she made her way through the darkened house, opened the sliding doors in the family room, and went out to the patio. She waited there, in one of the wrought-iron chairs, for her brother.

In a moment J.P. appeared in his baggy pajamas and bare feet. "It's the middle of the night, Caroline," he said. "This better be important. Because I don't get out of bed in the middle of the night for trivia."

"It is important, J.P.," Caroline told him. "I've wrecked everything. It's much worse than when I flushed the asparagus down the john. I've caused a very major, major catastrophe this time."

J.P. opened his eyes a little wider. "Was that YOU who flushed the asparagus?"

"FORGET THE ASPARAGUS! I need help, J.P.! I need advice. Maybe I even need lawyers."

"Why? I fixed up the computer situation, so Dad and Lillian aren't bankrupt. And you told me you fixed up the baseball team situation, so the Tater Chips have a shot, at least, at winning their game. What else is left?"

"The babies," Caroline said miserably.

"What about them?"

"Ivy has an earache and a fever, and so Lillian is taking her to the doctor in the morning for a penicillin shot."

"So? Big deal. Everybody gets penicillin shots now and then."

"Some people are allergic to penicillin," Caroline pointed out in an ominous voice. "*Holly* is allergic to penicillin."

J.P. sighed. "My feet are getting cold," he said. "Caroline, you're not making any sense. Holly's allergic to penicillin. Okay. If Holly had an earache, then, they wouldn't give her penicillin; they'd give her something else. But you already said that *Ivy* has the earache. So what's the problem?"

Caroline began to cry again. "It isn't Ivy," she sobbed. "That was my revenge. I switched the babies!"

FOURTEEN

CAROLINE HAD EXPECTED, somehow, that when she said aloud what she had done, thunder would boom, lightning would pierce the sky, and maybe the earth would open and swallow her up.

But none of that happened. The late-night breeze continued to rustle the leaves on the trees in Herbie and Lillian's yard. That was all.

J.P. huddled on his chair and wrapped his arms around himself against the chilly air. He gave an exasperated snort, and Caroline could see the look on his face, even in the dark. It was his "Anyone could have told you that" look.

"Caroline," he said with a resigned tone, "switch them back. It's that easy."

"No," said Caroline, "it isn't. I wish it were."

"Okay, so if you switch them back, then the one who has the earache is Holly. And Holly is allergic to penicillin. So you have to explain to Lillian that they were switched, and that's embarrassing, I grant you. But at least you don't end up giving penicillin to the wrong baby. That would be *worse* than embarrassing. That would be homicide, I think."

"The problem is, I'm not sure which one is which."

"Huh?" J.P. peered at her through the dark. "I thought you said you switched them."

Caroline tried to explain. It had seemed logical to her at the time. Now it just seemed insane. "I made up my mind to do it so that I wouldn't know which was which. So that I couldn't change my mind and undo it."

"How do you mean?"

"It was yesterday morning. You were off at baseball practice, and I was feeling sorry for myself because I was home alone with the babies, and I'd been thinking about doing it, and you said you had already done *your* revenge—"

"Yeah. When I wrote out my game strategy for tomorrow's game. I programmed them to lose."

"—and so after their breakfast, when they had oatmeal in their hair as always, I gave them each a bath in the kitchen sink, and washed their hair, and then—"

"Then what? Did you switch them or not?"

Caroline sighed. "I put them both in the playpen naked. Then I went out in the back yard for a few minutes and looked at the bird feeder. And I went to the bathroom. And I watched a little bit of *Donahue* on TV. And then finally, after I'd ignored them for about half an hour, I went and looked. And I didn't know which was which. They weren't in the same places I'd put them. You know how they crawl around and roll and squirm."

"So what did you do?"

Caroline shrugged. "I picked up one and dressed it in yellow. And I picked up the other and dressed it in pink."

"So they could be the *right* babies—"

"—or the wrong," Caroline pointed out.

There was a long silence. "Boy, Caroline," J.P. said at last, "I have to hand it to you. It was fiendishly clever."

"And it can't be undone," Caroline reminded him in despair. "The guy at the store fouled up the computer as revenge—but you undid it. And you fouled up the baseball team as revenge—but I undid it.

"But *me*," she said mournfully, "I fouled up the babies as revenge. And no one can undo it."

"*Wrong*," said J.P. suddenly, and he stood up. "You've been saved by genius, Caroline!" He headed toward the house and pulled open the sliding door.

"Where are you going? What are you going to do?"

"Come on," whispered J.P. from the dark family room. "Let's see if we can do it quietly so that Dad and Lillian don't hear anything."

"Do *what*, J.P.?" Caroline tiptoed into the house

after him. *"Ouch,"* she said, when she stubbed her toe on the leg of the coffee table. "Where are you? I can't see anything!"

"I'm at the door to your bedroom," J.P.'s voice said through the dark. "I'm about to go in to the babies to conduct a musical audition."

Caroline caught up with him as he opened the bedroom door. "What are you talking about?" she whispered.

"Remember?" J.P. told her. "Only one of the babies can whistle. Holly can whistle. Ivy can only go 'Bpheeewwww.'"

Caroline slept a little later than usual in the morning. For a change, the twins didn't wake her at dawn. Of course, the twins had been up from two to two-thirty in the morning, having their whistling tested. No wonder they were sleeping late.

Caroline stretched and yawned and listened to the activity in the rest of the house. Poochie was singing. He had a terrible voice: off-key and loud. But it was a happy voice, at least; he was singing "Take me OOOUUUTT to the baaaalll game!"

She heard her father call, "J.P.? I'm going down to the store to get Caroline's cap and shirt; you want to come? You could check the computer one more time!"

She heard J.P. respond and leave with Herbie.

She could hear Lillian in the kitchen, talking to Poochie.

Finally she heard the babies stir and wake. In the pink crib, the pink-gowned baby wiggled and peered, grinning, between the bars at Caroline.

"Hi, Holly," Caroline said. "Give a little whistle?"

Holly puckered up and whistled shrilly.

"Good girl," Caroline told her.

"Ivy?" she asked and looked into the yellow crib. Ivy was awake, too, but pulling at her ear again and whimpering.

Caroline reached into the yellow crib and patted Ivy fondly. "You're going to the doctor this morning," she told the baby. "He'll fix your ear up.

"Hey," she added, still patting the baby, "how about a little whistle?"

Ivy tried. But she still could manage only "Bpheeewwww."

Caroline got up, put her bathrobe on, and picked up the babies. She was so expert now at baby care that she could carry both of them at the same time, one balanced on each hip.

"Morning, Lillian," she said when she got to the kitchen. "I haven't changed them yet. But I will in a minute."

She put the babies in the playpen and went back to the bedroom for two dry diapers. In the bedroom, she stood still for a moment and looked at the two cribs, empty now. According to the whistling test, the babies had not actually been switched at all. Ivy was still Ivy. And Holly was still Holly. Ivy would get her penicillin shot and would be okay.

But what if—

Just suppose that—

Caroline had to be absolutely certain. She loved the babies too much to take a chance.

"Lillian," she said, when she got back to the kitchen. "I have a confession to make."

Lillian looked at her quizzically. She was fixing the babies' orange juice.

Caroline took a deep breath. "Yesterday morning," she said, "I gave the babies each a bath in the sink and then I put them into the playpen together—"

Lillian handed a bottle to each baby. She took one of the diapers and began changing Holly. Caroline leaned over and started changing Ivy.

"—and, ah, when I put them in the playpen together, they didn't have any clothes on yet. I mean, I hadn't yet dressed them after their bath," Caroline went on apprehensively.

Lillian started to laugh. She fastened Holly's diaper, patted her padded behind, and stood up. "So they got mixed up?" she asked.

"Yes," Caroline whispered, terrified. "And, Lillian, I'm almost positive that they're straightened out. I can't show you while they have their bottles in their mouths. But Holly can whistle, and Ivy can't."

Holly, sucking on her orange juice, heard the word *whistle*. She let go of her bottle, puckered up, and whistled some orange juice into the air.

Lillian chuckled, wiped Holly's chin, and said, "I do it all the time, Caroline. Don't worry about it."

Caroline stared at her in astonishment. "You mix them up?"

Lillian nodded. "Sure. It's inevitable. The pink and yellow clothes are handy. But let's face it — you can't keep them dressed every second. There's bound to be a mix-up now and then."

"But how—?"

"Oh, there are several ways to tell them apart," Lillian explained. "Ivy has a tiny mole on the back of her right shoulder. But that's a nuisance, because you have to take her shirt off to find it. It's a little easier to check the backs of their heads. Their hair grows in different directions. Here, I'll show you on Ivy — she's finished her juice."

She picked up the twin in the yellow nightgown and gently smoothed the fine dark hair on the back of her head. "See how it grows around counterclockwise in a circle? This *is* Ivy, by the way, in case you were still worried, Caroline. Holly's hair grows the opposite way."

Caroline stroked the baby's hair. "I *was* worried," she confessed. "It didn't seem good enough, relying on a whistle."

At the sound of the word, Ivy puckered her lips. This time, instead of a "Bpheeewwww," she gave a piercing whistle, just as accomplished as her sister's.

Poochie looked up. "She learned just in time," he said. "Now they can *both* whistle when I hit a home run!"

FIFTEEN

IT WAS THE TOP of the sixth inning of a game that was only six innings long, and Caroline was exhausted but exhilarated. The Half-Pints were at bat, and the Tater Chips were ahead by one run. The score was 32 to 31. If the score held, the Chips would win. But the Half-Pints were at bat.

"I didn't know baseball games had such high scores," J.P. remarked. He was sitting beside her on the bench, as assistant coach. "I thought that was football."

"It usually is," Caroline said. "But when nobody can catch, a lot of runs score. I forgot that the other team would be six-year-olds, too. They're just as bad as the Chips."

She was whispering so that the three players on the bench wouldn't hear. But they weren't listening, anyway. They were yelling insults to everyone who was wearing a uniform: to the players on the other team as they came to bat and to their own players who were out in the field.

"You can't catch, poophead Jason!" one little Tater Chip yelled to his own team's first baseman.

"Can too!" Jason yelled back just as the Half-Pints' batter hit a line drive toward first base. The ball went between Jason's legs and rolled toward right field.

Eric the Beaver was ready for it. It was amazing. At every practice, Caroline had watched as Eric had missed ball after ball because he always seemed to be doing some odd sort of ballet out in the field. She hadn't understood it until she had read her brother's revenge game plan.

"Eric the Beaver," his page had said. "Losing strategy: Supply with soda between innings. Do not suggest bathroom."

Caroline had simply cut off Eric's Pepsi supply and had ordered him to the men's room after each inning. Now, instead of prancing and twirling in the field, the Beaver was alert and attentive. He had already caught two fly balls and had dropped only one.

As she watched, cheering, Eric grabbed the ground ball. With his buckteeth firmly grabbing his bottom lip, he looked around for the runner, who had just passed first base. Jason, angry because the ball had gone between his legs, tried to trip him; but he missed, stumbled over his own foot, fell, and started to cry.

Eric threw to second, where Adam Donnelly was waiting.

"Adam Donnelly," his page in J.P.'s book had said. "Uses his brother's hand-me-down left-handed glove. Don't tell him he needs a right-handed glove."

Caroline had just convinced Adam and Poochie

to trade gloves. Poochie was left-handed and hadn't known it. Adam was the reverse.

Now, wearing Poochie's old glove, Adam leaned down and, with his left hand, scooped the ball successfully into the glove.

"WAY TO GO, ADAM!" yelled Caroline. But Adam looked around, confused. He was quite a distance from second base. The runner ran past him and reached the grubby bag that was the base marker. Panic-stricken, Adam threw the ball at the runner. It missed and rolled. The runner headed on toward third base, and the ball bobbled haphazardly across the bumpy infield toward the pitcher, Matthew Birnbaum.

Matthew was the Tater Chips' star player. He could hit, throw, and catch. There were no losing instructions on Matthew's page at all, except: "This kid can do everything. Have him bat first, when no one is on base. And substitute a bad player whenever possible."

Caroline had ignored that. She had made Matthew starting pitcher, and she had him batting cleanup, after three other batters, so that maybe he could help the others score. So far, in five and a half innings, he had scored twenty-seven other players, plus a few home runs all his own.

Now he scooped up the runaway ball and yelled, "Heads up, Poochie!"

Caroline cringed. Poochie was her third base-man. The sun was directly in his eyes, but it didn't matter, because Poochie was blind as a bat anyway. The only thing he had going for him was Adam Donnelly's brother's outgrown lefty glove.

Matthew tossed the ball to Pooch as the runner closed in on third base.

"COME ON, DAVID TATE!" Caroline bel-lowed.

Poochie squinted toward the sun, squeezed his eyes completely closed, and held his arms up awk-wardly. For the very first time, the ball landed in his glove.

And the runner, who should have been out at first, but wasn't, and who should have been out at second, but wasn't, ran right into Poochie's outstretched arm. Out at third, compliments of David Herbert Tate. He stamped his foot angrily and stalked off the field.

Two outs now. One to go, and the Tater Chips would win.

But the Half-Pints brought up their power hitter: Charlie Ping, a Chinese American kid with a punk haircut and muscles that looked obscene on a six-year-old. Charlie Ping had already hit, in this game alone, five grand slams.

Matthew Birnbaum took aim and pitched. *Whoosh.* Charlie Ping had his first strike of the day. Every other time at bat, he'd hit the first pitch.

Whoosh. Caroline couldn't believe it. The parents and brothers and sisters in the bleachers were going wild. She could hear Herbie Tate's booming voice: "That's two, Birnbaum! Strike him out!"

Matthew Birnbaum took a deep breath and pitched. But his pitching arm was tired, and his luck had run out. Charlie Ping swung a third time and connected with a splat that probably could be heard in downtown Cincinnati, three states and a large river away. The ball sailed up and away and over the fence.

Ping jogged, smirking, around the bases while the scorekeeper recorded the run. At least no one was on base. But now the score was tied: 32 to 32.

A little black kid with too big sneakers came up to bat, struck out, burst into tears, and was led away to be consoled by the Half-Pints' coach.

Now it was the Tater Chips' turn at bat, and one run would do it for them. *One run.* Caroline called a brief time-out and sent them, all but Kristin, to the men's room. All she needed was Eric the Beaver, who was up next, to start his ballet dance in the batter's box.

He didn't. He swung with enough energy to send a slam to the next county, but the bat only caught the edge of the ball and hit an odd little bouncing drive toward first base. The pitcher ran for it, collided with the first baseman, and they both fell down. Eric the Beaver could have made it to first base in the confusion. But he tripped over an untied shoelace; while he sprawled on the baseline, the ball rolled past; Eric picked it up politely and handed it to the first baseman.

Eric the Beaver was out.

Hastily Caroline ordered her remaining players: "Check your shoelaces!" J.P. jumped from his seat and went down the line on the bench, retying everyone's sneakers.

If only she could put Matthew Birnbaum in to bat. He could get the run that would win the game. But Matthew's turn wouldn't come for six more players.

Jason, the first baseman, was next. Caroline sighed. Jason had struck out every time at bat. Jason swung at everything: high balls, low balls, wild pitches, butterflies, and blowing leaves. Once someone had tossed a candy wrapper on the field when Jason was at bat, and he had swung at that.

Whoosh, whoosh, whoosh. Jason struck out so quickly it might have qualified for a world record. He was used to it; but he came back to the bench with his lower lip quivering, anyway.

And now Poochie—David Tate—was up.

"If only he had his glasses," Caroline muttered to J.P. "He can't even see to the pitcher's mound."

"He's gutsy, though," J.P. whispered back. "It takes a lot of guts to be a blind ballplayer."

Poochie marched toward the batter's box and aired a few theatrical practice swings. Then he took his place and assumed his batting stance, with his behind stuck out and his face scrunched up.

"No, Pooch!" Caroline yelled. "I mean David! You're backwards!"

Poochie remembered. He switched from right to left. At least he had a chance if he batted left-handed. Sometimes, just by accident, the ball bumped into the bat.

And it did this time. An aimless, looping pitch somehow casually ran into Poochie's awkwardly held bat, and Poochie moved the bat a little bit so that the ball reversed its direction and went out into the field. A few feet, at least.

"A bunt!" yelled Caroline. "Run, Pooch!"

Poochie squinted, trying to see where first base was. But he had lost his sense of direction when he switched from right-handed batting to left. He ran toward third.

The pitcher picked up the ball from where it lay in the dust. He walked it over to first base, handed it to the first baseman, and turned away with a smug smile.

But the first baseman dropped it and it rolled.

The crowd in the bleachers went wild.

Poochie, who had just begun to realize he was running in the wrong direction, had stopped in confusion and embarrassment. Now the crowd cheered him on. "Go the other way, Tate!" they yelled.

Poochie trotted back to home plate, looked around, got his bearings, and headed for first.

The first baseman had run after the dropped ball and collided with the second baseman, and now they were in the middle of a fistfight. The pitcher, who had started back to the mound thinking the game had ended in a tie, looked around, startled, then ran after the ball and picked it up. Now he and Poochie were both heading in a dead heat for first base.

And Poochie got there first. Angrily the pitcher heaved the ball out toward right field. But the right fielder had headed over to the sideline to buy an ice cream from the cart that was parked there.

The pitcher stomped, sulking, back toward the mound. The first baseman and the shortstop were both on the ground now, wrestling, biting, and kicking.

The right fielder was licking his ice cream sandwich and waving to his mother, who was aiming a camera at him from the bleachers.

And the ball rolled on and on.

Poochie began to run. When he rounded second base and headed toward third, the center fielder responded to the roaring instructions from the crowd and headed after the ball.

Poochie touched third base and the third baseman, a girl with two ponytails, stuck out her tongue at him as he passed.

The center fielder threw the ball toward the pitcher. But the pitcher was sulking, with his back turned, and didn't see it coming. The catcher ran in, picked it up, stumbled over an unbuckled strap from his too big chest protector, and fell, causing a cloud of dust to rise.

When the dust cleared, Poochie was standing on home plate, looking triumphant.

"I hit a home run!" Poochie yelled. "I told you I would!"

And the game was over.

SIXTEEN

Dear Mom, Caroline wrote. I'm sorry I haven't written all week. Forget everything I said in my first letter, anyway. Everything is all switched around.

Lillian has quit her real estate course, so I don't have to babysit anymore. And Ivy's earache is all better. Did I tell you that poor little Ivy had an earache?

So now that I am not babysitting, I am coaching David's baseball team. Did I tell you that Poochie's real name is David?

J.P. is working at Herbie Tate's Sporting Goods, running Dad's computer for the summer. Did I tell you that Dad has a computer?

In his spare time, J.P. is trying to teach the twins to whistle "The Battle Hymn of the Republic." Did I tell you that the twins can whistle? Isn't that the most amazing thing? And J.P. doesn't seem to mind that they spit when they whistle.

Lillian says that there is a museum in Des Moines after all—I thought there wasn't—and she will take me to it sometime, whenever I want to go.

But I'm not sure I'll have time. We have a big game coming up against the Squirts. We have a chance of becoming champions. And Poochie, I mean David, will have his glasses by the next game.

Did I tell you that Poochie needed glasses? And was left-handed so he needed to be switched around? And that was the whole, entire problem, right there.

Now that everything is switched around, J.P. and I actually like Des Moines quite a bit. Wait till you see the shirts that we will bring back to New York at the end of the summer.

They say:

MEET YOUR FATE
WITH HERBIE TATE

and they come in all sizes, even Adult. So if you would like one, just let me know and I can get it at a discount.

Or jogging shoes, if you'd prefer.

Love,
Caroline

Just the Tates!

Read all the books about Caroline and J.P.!